MW01132618

REMO WENT OFF

MIKE MCCRARY

To Remo. Such an asshole.

WHERE WE LAST LEFT REMO & FRIENDS

Remo checks the window.

More of a formality than anything. He knew what he'd see out there, but just needed to see it with his own eyes. They haven't started shooting or busting down the door yet. That's a good sign.

Maybe.

They have all their guns pointed at the house, scanning the windows and the doors, but they haven't opened up on him yet. They're waiting for something. *But what?* They know damn well Remo is in here alone. So why not finish this thing? Remo sees another man step out from the last car.

Remo realizes why, now.

A tall, slender man with hair cut close to the skull moves toward the house. He nods as one of the bad dude dildos tells him something. The slender man slides on some shades and moves with the swagger of a man without a care in the world and a dick the size of King Kong. He's dressed in a casual, cool style that cost him thousands. Remo is a little annoyed with the fact that even at a time like this he can calculate the cost of this guy's outfit. Holdover from his former life. *Can't help it,* he tells himself.

Remo knows this guy.

Hates this guy.

Used to have this guy as a client.

Justin Slim. J. Slim they call him. He is a man similar to Hollis. A contract killer, but with only one client, and that client is what has Remo moments away from pissing his pants.

"Remo," J. Slim calls out.

Remo says nothing, checks the AR.

"Remo, I know you can hear me. So I'll keep talking even if you don't return the favor."

J. Slim pauses on the off chance Remo will give up his position and he can go grab a drink and screw a local.

"Ray's not happy, as you can probably guess. Sure you've got a few former clients who feel the same," J. Slim says. "You fucked up, Remo. You really did. I don't know if you did us like you did the Mashburns..."

Remo opens the door a crack and bounces back, hoping he's not cut down by a storm of lead. When the bullets don't fly, he leans by the edge of the door and calls out, "I didn't do shit to Ray or you, motherfucker."

J. Slim cracks a smile. *Ahhh, Remo.* "Yeah, but the problem now is, how can we trust you? I mean every little thing that's gone wrong they can now pin directly on you, right or wrong. You see?"

Remo shuts his eyes tight. *Shit.* Cormac has made Remo the perfect scapegoat for every criminal organization on the planet.

How did the cops find us? Remo.

How did that get so fucked up? Remo.

Who took our fucking money? Remo.

Who did the thing about the thing? Remo.

"What do you do here, Remo? We're outside town, but not that far. If we start blasting it out with you the cops will eventually come and that doesn't do anybody any good. Think about it. You're hunkered down on a property with two dead CIA agents. That won't play well."

Remo bites his lip.

Thinks of Sean.

Thinks of putting a bullet in J. Slim and starting this thing off. If he can drop J. Slim he can start picking off the rest one by one, then jack one of these cars and get gone before the small-town, law-and-order mutts show up for the party. Remo can't believe this is how mutated his thinking has become. He used to think about suit fabric, good scotch and pussy. Now he's plotting mass murder at a CIA safe house, with an escape plan to boot.

Never stop learning, he thinks.

He takes aim on J. Slim's head. Fingers the trigger.

He can envision J. Slim's head bursting like a melon.

"I don't want a bloodbath here, Remo. I don't," J. Slim says, then motions to one of his bad dude dildos. "I can't see a way this ends with you alive, but I can make it as painless as possible."

The bad dude dildo takes something from J. Slim and moves toward the front of the house. Remo watches him holster his gun and walk to the front door. Remo positions himself behind a couch and takes aim at the front door. He waits for the firestorm to come.

It doesn't.

He hears the boots and footsteps patter as they move away from the house, followed by the sound of car doors closing. Out the window Remo watches the cars back up and leave the driveway. Only dirt in the wind.

Remo moves around the house checking all the windows. Looking to make sure there wasn't some dildo left behind to take Remo out when his guard is down. He gives the place a few good scans but doesn't find anyone.

Remo takes a deep breath and opens the front door wider.

Just a crack more, letting him get a peak of what's outside.

The dirt yard is empty. Only a plant that's barely alive and a three-legged dog hobbling down the gravel road barking at him. At his feet on the faded *Welcome Home* mat is an iPad with a Post-it note stuck on the screen.

There's a New York street address printed on the Post-it, along with the words, *Tap then meet us here!*

Remo's stomach drops through the ground before he even taps the screen.

With a single touch of his finger a video image of Sean and Anna playing at a park appears in crystal-clear HD. They are playing at a park Remo knows well. The same park Remo stumbled into after his battle in the Hamptons. Sean is laughing and running. Anna is chasing. Remo can't help but want to smile, but a tear rolls instead.

The camera turns around to face the man who's filming them. Remo doesn't recognize the man, but he knows the look. Sharp-dressed criminal. A high-net-worth asshole who's been upped from street murder boy to Manhattan resident based on his body count. Remo also recognizes the look in his eyes.

This guy is a killer.

This man enjoys the pain of others.

This man waves to the camera.

To Remo.

THE CHAOS OF ALL THAT SHIT

Part I

CHAPTER ONE

Remo is one fucked up slab of humanity.

He stares at the iPad for what seems like an hour. He knows it's only a few seconds, a minute tops, but it feels like an eternity. He simply stands there, helpless, watching a glass screen. Watching a killer while that killer watches his family. Remo is armed to the teeth, but powerless to do anything from his current position.

His finger tickles the trigger of his gun.

He allows his tired mind to wander.

A flash of a fantasy zips through his mind. A necessary break from reality. A much-appreciated defense mechanism. This private fantasy moment. The fantasy of pulling the trigger and removing whomever this motherfucker is off the planet. It provides Remo some comfort at least.

He shakes his head hard, trying to get right.

No time for this shit.

Setting the iPad down, he walks the room. With each passing moment, the pace becomes more and more manic. Back and forth. Sideways. Circles. Figure eights. A pause, then quick bursts of steps, then stopping suddenly and leaning against the wall with his head down. He needs a plan, an idea, an idea of a plan of what in the hell he can do make this all better. If only there were a pill to swallow to make this all go away. A button to unfuck himself. A way to undo the good deed of his that started this whole shitshow in the first place.

What was he thinking?

He had a good life.

A great life.

And he dicked it all up when he grew a conscience and decided to double-cross the Mashburn brothers after he saw some security camera footage. A slice of video that changed everything. He'd seen thousands of hours of security camera footage over the years mind you, but this particular footage on this particular day set a fire inside Remo that is currently burning down his life and everyone else's in it.

Remo's eyes blink as if clicking through a presentation.

He throws the Mashburn case.

Mashburns get pissed and come after him.

He gets into a massive bullet-ballet that leaves the Mashburns dead.

Most of them.

CIA gets their hooks into Remo.

They dig in deep by going through Detective Harris of the NYPD, who hates Remo with a passion. CIA boy Cormack—who's dead in a truck outside by the way—puts the screws to Remo and his boys, Hollis and Lester, to do Cormack's dirty work.

This included an unpleasant time with Mr. Crow, and taking down a heavily armed compound in the New Mexico mountains.

After slipping out of that disaster, Remo finds out Cormack put his thumb down on Remo because Remo pissed off Cormack's sister, and now Remo is in a CIA safe house with CIA dead bodies, guns and an iPad showing streaming footage of a psycho asshole eyeballing his family. Well, former family. Anna and he are divorced but he still cares about her, not to mention his son is really the thing that made Remo look at that security footage in a different, more human way to begin with.

Remo's head is a swirling mess of confusion, fear and regret.

No easy answers are coming his way. None out there to be found.

He rubs his gun as if rubbing a lantern in hopes a genie will appear and grant him three wishes. Hell, one good one would be nice. Then it hits him. It's a fragment of an idea at first. In his mind, Remo starts moving, sliding pieces into place. They don't all fit, mind you, but there are at least some pieces to work with. He knows what has to happen. The only shot he's got.

How do you start the million-mile journey?

By taking the first step.

Remo grabs the iPad, the note with the NY address, and a couple of guns and flies out the door. He opens the truck, letting Cormack's lifeless body drop to the driveway. The driver's side is a pulpy, bloody mess, but so is Remo. He can't feel most of his body and he's not completely sure how he's even able to walk. No time for self-examination. He'll go until he can't. Until he collapses or sees a long tunnel with a white light at the end. Remo slides in, literally, and sets his stuff down in the floorboard. As he fires up the engine he catches a glance of himself in the mirror.

It's not good.

Dark bags hang under his bloodshot eyes. Fresh blood is mixed with dried wounds from recent battles. They are a maze of reds and browns, indistinguishable as to where one begins and the next one ends. He can see the crazy in his own eyes. He used to have the calm eyes of an attorney who had the world by the nuts. Now the world has his in a tightly held, unkind grip.

He slaps himself.

Finds a classic rock station on the radio.

Cranks it up and jams the gear in R.

He slams on the brakes as a three-legged dog passes by the back bumper.

Remo hopes like hell he can remember how to get back.

How to get back to the Mashburn compound nestled up in the mountains.

CHAPTER TWO

Winding up the mountain everything looks the damn same.

Every tree. Every rock. Every twist and turn in the road reveals the same thing. He has no idea where he is going. The trip down the mountain with Cormack was only an hour ago, but it was a blur. Remo had been beaten, shot at and held at gunpoint while CIA man Cormack explained how he'd truly ruined Remo's life. The information came at him a like a sledgehammer. Each word hitting harder than the next. Every syllable explaining how Remo was a dead man. So, Remo wasn't exactly paying attention to the way he came down the mountain.

Maybe he's seen that sign before.

Maybe.

Don't know, not for sure.

All he does know is he needs to go up. The Mashburn compound was up the mountain, so if he heads that way he will at least be moving in the right direction. Blind-ass progress is better than no progress at all.

The serpent-like road dead-ends.

He backs up and takes another route that leads him up.

Up is good, he thinks.

He reaches an RV park. Doesn't remember seeing it before. Wrong way. He hits R again and takes another path that wraps around and up the mountain. It's all too much. He can feel himself coming undone. This needle in the haystack feeling is crushing what's left of his battered, fragile psyche. Every wood house looks the same. Every mountains-vacation family looks the same. Every stone. Every tree. Every hand-carved wooded bear looks the damn same.

Up and up he goes. The old truck pushes farther and farther up the mountain like an aging climber driven beyond reason. Remo's mind is on fire. His thoughts collide, spin, flip then burst into flames. None of his ideas or memories are connecting into anything he can use. He's only processing fear and darkness. There's no great way out of this and he knows it. This will end with people dying. He can only hope it's not Sean and Anna.

He glances to the iPad. Its screen has long since gone dark. He made the wise decision not to look at it while trying to navigate the mountain road. Didn't see the value in it. He is, of course, appreciative that J. Slim and company gave him one with cell service rather than just Wi-Fi, so he can watch wherever he goes. So thoughtful, those folks. He looks to the black screen. Can't help but think about what's going on in the darkness of that glass. Just a harmless advance in tech resting on a seat, but yet it holds all the hopes and fears Remo has.

He can't help himself.

He swipes the screen.

He checks the road. Clear.

The screen lights up. The whacko killer is following Anna and Sean. Now they are on the streets of New York. This is new. It's a jerking, bouncing, camera style footage with the images moving back and forth with his walking, but it's plain to see that he is following them wherever they go.

Remo feels sweat forming on the back of his neck. His mouth goes dry.

He realizes he has to get to New York fast. He has no idea how to get there or what the smartest or best way to do it is, but he cannot continue to watch from afar like this. This is unbearable, and that's probably the point. He realizes that was the plan. He realizes that's what J. Slim and Ray want.

He realizes he hasn't looked at the road in a long time.

Remo looks up.

Locks the brakes.

He sees something strangely familiar. Something he most definitely recognizes. Remo smacks his lips. Blinks. Stares in disbelief. Seems like years ago, but it was actually earlier today when he last saw it.

Cracking a sly grin, Remo points a finger gun at a Yukon parked on the side of the mountain road.

"Gotcha."

CHAPTER THREE

He, Hollis, Lester and Cloris left the Yukon there not long ago.

Feels like a lifetime ago.

Remo's heart skips a beat or six. He's close. They have to be around here somewhere. His memories flood in fast like a tsunami. All of it. The house. The chicken pepperoni fight between Hollis and Cloris. Cloris and Lester. Cloris and everyone. The chaos of all that shit. The blood. The three of them fighting, arguing while hiking up the mountain.

Remo grinds his teeth. *Holy shit he's close*.

The compound has to be up just a bit farther. Thinking hard, he remembers there was a second driveway that big Mexican Mountain bastard and his angry-ass friends drove into before they started with the shooting and all that shit. There has to be another way up, one he can drive. He doesn't have time to hoof it up the side of the mountain the way he and Cloris did earlier today.

His eyes dart left and right looking for a way. A path. Something that will show him the fastest route to the compound. Out of the corner of his eye he sees something.

It's not a faster route.

Not a road.

Not a path of least resistance.

It's something rolling. Falling. Tumbling down the mountain through the trees. Rumbling awkwardly without much style or sense of direction. Remo looks harder. He makes out a rolling mass of arms and legs. A whirling dervish of fists and feet that starts and stops, then moves down only to stop again. A ball of elbows, anger and red faces locked in hate.

Cloris, Hollis and Lester are fighting like hell, wrapped around each other while falling down the mountain. Remo can't believe what he's seeing. This misplaced tumbleweed of hostility coming his way. He watches as one breaks off from the other two, stumbles, then jumps back in. It's hard to determine who's on whose side. There seems to be no real winners or losers here.

A threesome of violence as opposed to lust.

Remo opens the creaky truck door and steps out. Stops and then grabs a gun. Just in case Cloris is still in the mindset of killing Remo. He walks up cautiously, trying to devise a plan as he moves closer. In very quick order he runs through the possibilities of what he should do here. He could shoot one of them, probably Cloris, but that might set off Lester. He'd rather not hurt any of them. They've been through a lot recently, especially him, Hollis and Lester. Okay, fine, he won't shoot anyone. Unless of course Cloris tries to shoot him. Remo is still on the fence as to what the hell Cloris's big plan is here. She probably doesn't have one. If she does, it probably resets from minute to minute as her crazy-ass mind clicks and clacks its way through life. Her love for Lester seems to be the constant. Her unhealthy, destructive, crazy-as-hell love for Lester.

They've reached a flat part of land. A "landing spot," if you will. They are about thirty feet ahead of Remo, still giving him some room to operate and think. For the first time Remo can make out what's happening.

Hollis swings a backhand toward Cloris.

She ducks and lands a jab to his kidneys. He alters his swing and ends up tagging Lester in the eye. Maybe by mistake, but it doesn't stop Lester from taking a full swing that misses Hollis and crunches Cloris square in the jaw.

Hollis slumps to a knee.

Cloris spins to the ground.

Lester is straight-up staring at Remo. Confusion washes over his dirty, bloody face. He looks back toward the mountain, then to Remo, then to the truck with the cracked windshield, blown-out passenger window and blood slopped everywhere. His eyes move back to Remo.

"How'd you get here, friend?" Lester asks, trying to catch his breath.

"Long story, friend," Remo replies.

"Can't be that long. We just been fighting for an hour or so, tops."

"A lot can happen in an hour."

Lester nods.

Cloris stands up, as does Hollis. They both take defensives stances but don't attack. More out of exhaustion than anything. Rage burns hot and fast, but doesn't last. Not at these levels. Hollis spits out a wad of blood and dirt. Cloris tries to hold Lester's hand. He pulls away. Cloris does her best to hide her hurt, but she sucks at it. Suppressing emotions isn't her strong suit. She twirls her head to pop her aching neck, then crosses her arms, then allows a finger to twirl a strand of hair.

Remo has no idea where to start, but knows he has to. He wanted so badly to be the leader at the beginning of today, and now he knows he has to be a good one if he is going to have any chance of finding Anna and Sean. There's no time to read a best-selling book on management, filled with pyramids and blah-blah about paradigm shifts and top-ten lists of heady horseshit that in the real world equates to blank stares and jokes behind your back at the water cooler. Still, Remo needs to find a way to get these people on board. Needs to find a button to push within them to get these three masters of mayhem up for battle one more time. Perhaps one last time.

Does he go with a big speech?

Honest begging?

Crying?

Remo realizes more than a moment of silence has passed since they stopped beating the piss out of one another. All three of the battered, beaten members of his *team* are looking at him. Waiting. Waiting for something out of Remo. Anything Remo has to offer. They don't have any answers. If they did, they wouldn't have spent their time fight-falling down a mountain. They continue to stare at Remo as their breathing starts to even out.

Remo simply clucks his tongue like Cormack used to do. Well, before Remo blew his brains all over the truck behind him.

"Looks like you've got something on your mind," Hollis says, breaking the silence.

"That I do, Hollis," Remo says, scratching his nuts with his gun. "That I do."

CHAPTER FOUR

Remo does his best to explain what in the hell has happened since they last saw him at the Mashburn compound.

There's a lot.

More than Remo would like.

He tells them about Cormack and how he fucked all of them over. Mainly Remo, but they are all involved. CIA man Cormack let it slip out to the greater part of the US criminal community that Remo ratted out the Mashburn brothers. He more or less told every thug, murderer and criminal overlord that Remo threw a case and had the Mashburns sent to prison. Not to mention Remo also took the Mashburns' money from a bank robbery. Cormack probably left out the part where Remo gave (most of) it to charity. This info leak thus started off a shitstorm of other criminals thinking Remo might have or will do the same to them.

That's what caused the larger issues at the Mashburn compound. The uninvited guests. The Mexican Mountain and his friends who stormed in with guns blazing. Remo tables his concerns over Cloris chopping off her father's head—doesn't see the need to open that can of worms—but he does talk about killing Cormack and another CIA agent at the CIA safe house and the little chat he had with J. Slim. Remo even goes as far as to show them the iPad, which now has the psycho watching Anna and Sean's apartment from across the street.

"I know J. Slim," Hollis says. "He's a fucking asshole."

Remo nods in agreement. No need to say more. No need to dig up all that.

"Like to put a bullet or ten into him and Ray." Hollis continues talking, seeming to get more and more worked up with each word. "But since he brought Anna and Sean into this thing of ours, I'll make their deaths slightly less humane."

Remo smiles with appreciation.

He was hoping Hollis would take this point of view. Perhaps managing by doing and saying less is the answer here. Let them fill in the gaps. Let their brains work it through rather than tell them what to think. He turns to Lester and Cloris, but says nothing. There's a sting of silence. The wind blows. The trees shift, limbs swaying in the breeze.

Cloris looks to Lester. Lester looks to Remo.

"I'd like to help you," Lester says. "If you'll still have me."

Remo lets a sigh escape. A wave of relief rolls over him. He knows it's silly to get emotional about a completely insane, Jesus-freak killer choosing to join him on a half-baked mission leading them to almost-certain death, but Remo can't help but get a little choked up.

"Of course," Remo says. "And thank you."

Lester nods.

"You fucking kidding me?" Cloris says.

The silence is back. The wind blows.

"You're more than welcome to join," Remo says through clenched teeth. "Of course we'd need to resolve a few issues beforehand."

"Like?" she says.

"Like, say, I don't know, the fact you tried to kill me about an hour ago."

"That's the past."

"Not very distant past."

"The past nonetheless."

Remo lets it go, clucks his tongue. Now he can't stop doing it.

Cloris takes Lester's face in her hands. "What do you want me to do?" Lester looks down. Cloris raises his face to meet her eyes. "Tell me, baby. What do you want?"

"What I've always wanted," Lester says. "For you to do what makes you happy."

Cloris slaps the shit out of him.

"Just fucking say you don't want me anywhere near you next time," she barks. "Don't be a snatch about it."

Hollis and Remo glance to one another, then let their eyes slide back to the unhappy couple. Lester doesn't even bother touching his pulsing face. He lets it throb and burn, or he doesn't even feel it, given the beatings they've taken and laid down on each other today.

"We can use your help," Remo chimes in, trying to appeal to Cloris. "I. Me. I can use your help."

Cloris lets her death stare whip over from Lester to Remo. She's listening, but there's no telling how she's processing the words that have been spoken to her. There's what's said and then there's the perception of those words, and trying to guess how the words will translate in that meat grinder of a head is a fool's errand.

Remo resets and starts again.

"They have my son and my ex-wife. Anna and Sean have nothing to do with any of this shit," Remo says. "They are completely innocent. Their only mistake was having me in their lives."

"Massive mistake," Cloris says.

Hollis can't help but chuckle. *You ain't kiddin'.*

"Be that as it may, " Remo continues, ignoring their bullshit, "I have to help them. I came back here for your help. I'm asking for your help. I'm willing to go it alone, but I can really use all of you."

Remo knows he's lying a bit. He really only wanted Hollis and Lester, and could give two shits if Cloris joins in or not. Actually, he thinks her leaving would be best, but he doesn't want to further escalate or reignite the violence between the four of them. He knows he needs to make this look good. He decides to add some more shine.

"I'll ask you again." Remo puts his best sincere face on display. "Will you help me—"

"Fuck you," Cloris says. She slaps the shit out of Lester again, kisses him with a sloppy tongue, then stomps his foot and plants a foot into his knee.

As Lester drops to the dirt she storms past Remo, giving him a lightning-fast thump to the nuts as she passes by. Remo buckles. As he twists to the ground he watches her tear off down the mountain in the opposite direction.

Hollis helps Lester up. They share a look, but don't bother speaking. What's the point? They've been through a lot in the last few days. Way too much to discuss. Cloris leaving is just another bullet point in a long list of questionable shit.

Remo sucks in a long breath, letting the queasiness in his stomach subside. Pulling himself upright, he looks to his boys. His brothers-in-arms. His team.

They share odd smiles.

Together again.

For better or worst.

"Okay, Remo," Hollis says, "you got us. What's your master plan?"

Remo starts to cluck his tongue again, but stops himself. He really doesn't know what his plan is, but he's got some fragments of ideas that might work. Anything is possible.

"Please tell us you've got something," Hollis says.

"Yeah, give us something, Remo," Lester says.

Remo holds up a finger. He needs to frame the sketchiness of this thing in a positive way or this new buy-in from them will dissolve rapidly. Words need to be well chosen. Structured properly and delivered with strength.

"We're going to..." Remo pauses. "I don't fucking know, but I've got some ideas."

Hollis and Lester actually seem surprised by his honesty. They were fully expecting layers upon layers of cascading bullshit to come raining down from Remo, but instead they got raw honesty. A new development. They appreciate the break for once. Remo picks up on the vibe and makes another mental managerial note.

Honesty and selective silence.

It works.

Who fucking knew?

CHAPTER FIVE

Remo, Hollis and Lester climb out of the Yukon.

Hollis had pulled up as close to the cabin as he could in case they needed to bounce the hell out of there at a moment's notice. They do a quick sweep around the place taking some quick peeks into the windows with guns drawn. They have no idea how many people really know about this place. Given what Cormack told Remo, it's hard to believe Cormack told anybody. The way Cormack explained it, he had this whole operation with Remo completely off the books and the only people who knew about it were now recently departed, their dead bodies littered in various places in New Mexico.

But.

But, Cormack could have told the world. Anything and everything is a possibility. He could have someone else in the CIA working this thing. Somebody they don't even know about. Not out of the questions at all. There's an off chance Detective Harris from New York might know a little, but Remo doesn't think Cormack would feed that dipshit much info. No upside for Cormack.

Once the place seems clear the three enter through the front

door. The place is exactly the way they left it. Some dishes and
shit still in the kitchen. The remnants of the chicken pepperoni
battle that raged last night. Some stained sheets from Lester and
Cloris's little afternoon delight. But that's about it.

They take seats on the couches in the living room. Wasn't
much talking on the ride over. The exhaustion of the last couple
of days is really hitting them hard. They all needed a minute to
reboot. To let the silence heal them a bit. Remo thinks of his lost
friends—Johnnie Walker Blue and his pills. Be nice if he could
reconnect with them some time soon.

He's pretty sure that time, violence and blood loss have helped
him detox, but Remo never asked to detox and was not, and still
is not, interested in giving either one of them up. After he gets
Anna and Sean safe and sound, the second order of business is to
get the pipeline of sauce and pills flowing again.

Remo pulls over checking the iPad. That psycho asshole is
still sitting watching the apartment. Remo tries to send mental
telepathy their way. *Stay in the apartment and out of sight. Do not let
anybody inside. Not without a fight.*

"We going to cut up a plan or not?" Hollis asks, breaking the
silence.

"Yeah, what's the word on this thing?" Lester adds.

Remo picks at the corners of an idea he had on the way over.
"Hollis, you remember J. Slim having a brother? A little one. A
little piece of shit asshole brother?"

Hollis thinks. "Sounds about right. Started with a D or
some shit."

"Yeah, D-something."

"David?"

"No."

"Desmond?"

"No."

"Douchebag?"

"Yes, but no."

They pause.

Remo's mind unspools. It's as if the hard drive in his skull is unloading data. He remembers J. Slim and his boss Ray and how they used to do business. J. Slim used to be a contract guy. Freelance killer, a lot like Hollis, which is how Hollis knows him. They traveled in similar circles. Both former military. Both competed for similar work. Then J. Slim went exclusive. Got a retainer, for lack of a better explanation, from a criminal superpower named Ray.

Just Ray.

No cool nickname or badass handle. Simply Ray, and Ray ran shit. He even ran Mr. Crow, and Mr. Crow's operations. Remo remembers Crow for a split second and how Remo, Lester and Hollis almost went down dealing with one of Crow's establishments only a couple of days ago.

Ray has had a paw in a lot of things, but the larger cash cows are drugs, guns and money. No big shocks there, but Remo did hear recently that Ray was big into counterfeiting. Counterfeiting foreign currencies in particular. Harder and harder to bullshit the US paper these days. Ray was working to perfect some of the third world, emerging markets stuff and then convert to dollars. Not a bad plan. Remo pieced this together based on some meetings he had with Ray's associates who came to Remo for legal services over the last year or so.

You see, Ray had Remo on retainer as well. Different from J. Slim, but similar.

All of this is to say Remo knows Ray moves a lot of things around the board. Tons of illegal tonnage pushed, pulled, bought and sold. Drugs, guns, money, both fake and real, and if Remo and his buddies can find a way to disrupt that or, better yet, steal some significant portion of it, then they can use it to leverage a way out for Anna and Sean.

Maybe.

Perhaps.

It's not a plan without risk, but it's the best one Remo has.

Remo explains his thoughts to Lester and Hollis and ties this idea back to that piece of shit, asshole D-something brother of J. Slim. That guy is the way to get in. That guy is the weakest link in a chain that is otherwise strong as hell. If they break D-something wide open, then they've got a chance.

Remo and Hollis know something else.

This D-something motherfucker is a junkie, and a junkie can be squeezed. More to the point, this D-something junkie can be squeezed hard by Hollis and Lester, and will sing like a canary. After the singing ends, Remo can find out where to hit Ray, but first they need to find this guy. Well, first they need to remember the little fucker's name.

"Duffy," Lester says.

Remo stops just short of telling him, *No*. He can't. Hollis and Remo look to one another. That's it. Lester's right.

"Do you know this guy?" Remo asks Lester.

"No," he says.

"Well," Hollis says, "how in the hell—"

"Was thinking of Cloris and I remembered a three-way we had once together and it was with this dude named Duffy." Lester sighs. "This was a while back. It's not your Duffy, because Cloris killed him after we were done. He made a rude comment about her. Something about a nipple. Anyway, that's what made me think of it."

Remo and Hollis blink. That's the most they've heard Lester say at one time.

"Glad I could help," Lester says.

CHAPTER SIX

It's a long road to NY from NM.

They can do it in a day if they ride hard straight through and if they don't mind destroying a few speed laws along the way. Remo thinks he has a day or so to work with. J. Slim knows damn well he can't roll with a commercial airline back to NYC. Not with the heat that's on him. Even a fucking asshole like him knows how the world works. This is why the psycho on the iPad is simply watching. All these things lead Remo to believe he has some time to get to New York. Also, the psycho on the iPad had held up a piece of paper with a date and time written on it. A time to meet.

It's in two days.

Remo, Lester and Hollis have loaded up the Yukon with the guns and money they took from Cormack. This gives them a somewhat respectable stash of weapons, ammo and cash. They know it's not enough. They know they need things. Things they don't have. They need more money if they are going to go after Ray. On a positive note, they have a good idea where to get some. They've decided to make a quick stop by the Mashburn compound. It's a risky-as-hell move, but they know it will be worth it.

Hopefully.

After much fighting and getting lost trying to find the way up the mountain, they pull up to the back gate. They've made it. They decide that one of them should stay by the Yukon and lay on the horn if any shit comes their way. Hollis draws the short straw and stays behind. Armed to the teeth, of course.

It's very strange being back here, Remo thinks. Granted it's only been about an hour or so, but stepping over the bodies, dodging the blood and all that can mess with a person's head. Even if that person is Remo Cobb.

They also know they have to be quick. There's no telling how fast people will come and check it out or how quickly Johnny Law will work its way up the mountain. They made a shitload of noise during that battle at the compound. Hard to believe it went completely unnoticed, but the isolated location does buy them some time.

Some time. Not an eternity.

The thinking was there might be some money or guns or at least something to eat at the compound that they could use. Money is a cure-all for some of the shit they might encounter and they know damn well they don't have enough it. As selfish as it sounds, Remo is secretly hoping there's some Johnnie Blue in the compound. He hates himself for even looking, but shit, man, the urge goes bone deep.

Remo wanted Lester to come along with him into the compound on the off chance he might have some familiarity with the place, considering Lester knew Daddy Mashburn better than he and Hollis did. Lester, of course, had no idea where to go once they got inside.

The place is massive in every direction. A truly jaw-dropping home, and it's a little hard to believe the Mashburns put this place together. It's like an upscale ski lodge. Stone fireplace.

Ceiling reaching to the heavens. Skylight letting the sun peek in, with rays bouncing off the hardwood floors and polished oak furniture.

They hit the kitchen first. Lester fills a Nike bag with some chips, drinks and shit. There's a fully cooked, five-pound brisket wrapped in foil centered in the fridge like a prized jewel in a museum. Big score. They also snag some potato salad and some forks.

Lester assumes that any money or anything of value would be hidden.

He's right.

Not only hidden, but protected.

There's a side wing to the compound. Just off the back part of the main house. Blacked out windows. Heavy door. Pretty damn obvious. Remo and Lester take positions on either side of the door. They share eyes and make a silent count to three. Remo tries the knob knowing damn well it won't work.

It doesn't.

He looks to his watch. They've been there about five minutes already. They wanted to be in and out in less than ten. Remo looks to Lester. Lester shrugs his shoulders. Remo shrugs his shoulders. He doesn't like being there this long. His look to Lester is almost trying to tell him, *Well, we tried. Let's get the hell out of here.*

Lester gets the signal, doesn't disagree, and he starts backing away.

A blast rips through the door.

Lester and Remo hit the floor face-first.

There's the faint sound of a shotgun pump from the other side of the door before another hole punches through.

Remo covers his head with his hands while turning to Lester. Lester springs up with his gun at the ready. He pushes his back against the wall to the right of the blown-out door. It's now quiet. Smoke from the shotgun blast twists and twirls into the air. Stink of gunpowder fills the room. There's an ever-so-slight rustling sound from inside the room.

"Dammit. Look," Remo calls out to whoever's in the room as he gets up, "we don't want a lot of shit. We just want to get out of here. No harm. No foul."

"Shut the fuck up," Cloris says, strolling out of the room with a bag in her fist and a shotgun leaning against her shoulder. She stops, standing between Remo and Lester. She looks them up and down then tags both of them in the dick with the butt of her shotgun. Remo and Lester drop to their knees.

"You pussies can have what's left," she says as she leaves.

From the ground, Lester and Remo can only watch her leave. She gives them the finger as she slips through the door and out of sight.

Remo has no idea what to say to Lester. Who would at a moment like this? She has punched him, nut thumped him, shot at him and left him all in the same day. This is new territory, even for Remo.

Remo goes with an understanding smile. Always a good move.

"Told you she'd kill us all," Lester says.

CHAPTER SEVEN

The longest part of the drive wasn't from New Mexico to New York.

It was when they hit NYC. It was a crawl. Remo kept an eye on the iPad, but to their word J. Slim's boy did not make a move. The connection was sketchy in spots along the trip. When they went dark outside New Mexico Remo's anxiety shot through the roof, but he was able to keep in good contact most of the way.

Oddly enough, there wasn't a whole lot of talk along the way. They took turns driving while at least one of them slept. The weight of the last few days had finally kicked all three of them in the teeth and they needed the time to decompress. As much as they could at least. There was a dicey moment when they thought they were going to get pulled over in Ohio, but thankfully the cop breezed on by.

They managed to get a decent take off the Mashburn compound. A fair amount of cash, and a stockpile of guns and ammo. They took it all, thinking that it might come in handy. You never know, but getting pulled over and explaining to cops why you're traveling with cash and an arsenal might prove challenging.

The ride also gave Remo some time to try and process this plan of theirs. It has holes you could drive a truck through, but it's what they've got to work with. Besides, in all the hours the trip has taken, Remo couldn't pull a more viable plan out of his ass.

Remo isn't completely sure where to find Duffy, but he's got a guess. The Jiggle Queen is a New Jersey strip joint and was a second home for young Duffy, if Remo remembers correctly. Or course Remo has spent some chunks of his life there as well. He tells himself it was all about business, and it was to a certain extent, but Remo enjoyed the flashes of bare skin and the smiles from ladies as much as the next poor slob.

Remo, Hollis and Lester haven't worked out the details yet, but they need to get Duffy to tell them what Ray has going on next. They need him to give up a money drop, a safe house, a card game, anything. Ray's operations are a flowing thing that roll in and out on a daily basis. Multiple moving parts. Things are always in constant motion. Remo needs one of those things. A thing that's got size. A thing that's big enough to get Ray's attention. Something that will hurt if it gets taken down and, oh yeah, they need it to happen today.

They enter the Jiggle Queen. The dark, open room is packed to the gills with desperation, driving beats and surgically enhanced grace twisting and grinding onstage. The air feels sweaty. The floor feels sticky. The money feels dirty. The three cut through the place like men on a mission. They are met by full-frontal nudity and fake smiles, but our boys pay them no mind. Well, not exactly no mind. They steal a quick eyeful, but the point is they don't stop and chat or get a dance for fuck's sake.

Scanning.

Searching.

They split up to cover the place. Remo watches with steely eyes. He takes in every face. Every drunken hope for companionship. Every twenty passed and every set of rolling eyes from the ladies. He glances toward the back.

His eyes pop.

He sees Duffy being led by the hand into a VIP room—the Jiggle Lounge. A separate room in the back for private dances at a price. Remo twirls his finger in the air, getting Hollis's and Lester's attention. He points to the Jiggle Lounge's closing door.

Hollis and Remo rush in. They leave Lester to stay outside and watch the door. He knows his role here. He's there to grease the bouncers with some flash cash if they come by, and also to keep any pain in the ass horndogs from trying to step in. Lester can use force only if necessary.

Destiny is not happy about her new guests arriving in the lounge. Her faux sweetness dissolves fast the second she sees Remo and Hollis enter. There are rules here, dammit.

"No. No. Fuck no," Destiny spits out in the thickest of Jersey accents. "You motherfuckers step the hell outta this motherfucker here. Not doing some weird group love..." She pauses. Scrunches her nose. "Remo?"

Remo nods. "Hi."

She's not happy to see him. She charges hard at him. Like a pissed off bull. Hollis grabs her by the shoulders, holding her back along with her swinging arms and kicking legs. She screams, but Hollis covers her mouth best he can.

"I know. I know." Remo steps up to her, trying to reason with her. "I don't have time for apologies and all that shit. Let's just say you're not happy with me and I don't remember why."

She screams louder through Hollis's fingers.

Duffy now realizes what's up and starts to move toward the door on the sly.

"Sit the fuck down," Hollis barks.

Duffy complies. His ass lands in a chair fast.

"Good boy." Remo turns his attention back to Destiny. "Go outside. There is a man by the door. He will hand you a stack of cash and you will happily go away from this room and tell no one who's in here. Take the rest of the day off. Enjoy yourself."

She calms a bit. Stops screaming.

Remo nods for Hollis to move his hand.

"Outside? How much?" she asks hard, then shifts to a purr. "Give me a number, hon."

"It's enough," Remo says, hoping that Lester has enough.

"Okay," she says as she kisses Hollis and Remo on the cheek then slinks out of the room like the temptress she was born to be.

As the door shuts, Remo and Hollis turn their attention solely to Duffy. If Duffy could crawl under the dirty, sticky floor he would. He shakes, tremors working overtime from his fingers to his toes. Remo can't tell if this is fear or if the kid needs a taste to get him right.

This reminds Remo of something.

Something important.

He sticks his head outside the door, finding Destiny dancing for Lester. Lester has a hundred folded and stuck between his teeth. Remo starts to comment and/or condemn the both of them, but instead he stays on task.

"Can someone get me a Johnnie Blue?" Remo asks.

He gets blank stares from the two of them. Destiny has her head between her legs looking up at him with a *what the fuck, I'm working here* expression. Remo snatches the hundred from Lester's teeth, hands it to her and points to the bar.

"Johnnie. Blue, please."

Stepping back into the room, Remo shuts the door. The hum of Mötley Crüe is rattling the walls. Remo loves this jam, but fights that shit. He has work to do here. Hollis already has Duffy wrapped into a human pretzel. Remo flips a steel chair around and takes a seat so that he's eye level with Duffy. Remo has seen this scene worked by cops over the years. Now it's his turn to give it whirl.

"Now, Duffy, what should we talk about?" Remo asks.

"What the hell, man?" Duffy spits and sputters. "I didn't do shit to you and this ape prick."

Hollis slaps him.

Not too hard, but hard enough to let Duffy know there's another level he can go to. Remo lets the sting take hold. Wants to make sure Duffy can even feel it and is not completely stoned to the point of numbness. Duffy's twisted expression of sharp pain and annoyance lets Remo know that Duffy is firmly planted in the here and now.

"We don't have a lot of time here," Remo says. "We've come a long way just to see you, my boy."

"Ooooo, to what do I owe the pleasure of your company? I heard you're a dead man," Duffy says.

Hollis slaps him harder, almost knocking him from the chair.

"Probably, but before they get to me I might take some time and watch Hollis hurt you for a while. Give me a little giggle before I get my ticket punched." Remo leans back. "Yeah, let me think on that. It is the little things I'll miss when I'm dead."

As if on cue, Destiny steps in with Remo's Johnnie Blue. She sticks it in his hand.

"No change," she says, leaving.

Remo becomes entranced. Lost while looking into the glass. It really hasn't been that long, but it feels like decades to Remo. He sniffs. The hairs on the back of his neck fire up. He touches his mouth to the edge of the glass, letting the booze touch his lips ever so gently. He pulls back. Taking a moment. Don't rush it, he thinks. Then he tilts the glass back, taking a long pull. It burns the good burn. Remo almost feels himself come back online. His brain slides into place. His soul realigns. Can't help but think of Popeye getting him some spinach. Remo is back, and not a moment too soon.

He forgets that he's not alone in the universe. Turning, he sees both Hollis and Duffy staring at him like he's out of his mind.

"Didn't think that I'd like to have something?" Hollis holds his hands out. "Maybe dear Hollis would like a drink?"

"Yeah, rude motherfucker," Duffy chimes in.

Hollis slaps Duffy again, this time sending him spinning out from the chair. Remo downs the rest of his magical elixir, then slams the empty glass down hard. Making sure he has Duffy's attention, he gets up and helps Duffy back up into his chair. As he does, Remo fixes his shirt, giving Duffy a look of compassion. It's complete bullshit, but Remo couldn't care less. It's all part of the game he's running here.

"Tell him to stand down, man," Duffy says, looking at Hollis with eyes bugging out.

"No, no I'm not going to let Hollis tear you apart," Remo says, petting Duffy's hair. "As entertaining as that would be, I'm going high road with this here. I'm going to let you help us instead."

Duffy adjusts his mouth, working the feeling back to it as Remo walks toward the back corner of the room as if he's pondering something deeply. Duffy doesn't like the sound of this at all. When a man like Remo tracks you down at a strip club in the middle of the day, it's usually not out of kindness. This man wants something, and it's more than likely not something you'd like to give. Duffy shifts in his seat. Waiting like a child for his medicine.

"I need something. A time and a place. I need a time and place of a money thing that J. Slim is doing for Ray," Remo says, moving closer to Duffy as he speaks. The Johnnie Blue is working through his system, healing as it goes. Remo is feeling his superpowers of bullshit returning with a vengeance. "What I want—sorry." He motions to Hollis and then himself. "What we want is for you to give us something we can use. That's all."

Duffy wiggles in his chair. Claws at his wrists and arms.

"I know there's something going on out there. Ray's always got some kind of cash moving around the board. Just tell me what's going on. Today, preferably. Maybe we can help each other."

Duffy's head perks up.

Remo raises his eyebrows while nodding, coaxing it out of him.

"See. I appreciate you working with me on this. Maybe, just maybe, there's something you know about that you'd like a piece of. Something for you." Remo is reading the story that Duffy's weak, pathetic face is telling him. His sagging, tired mug is speaking to Remo loud and clear. The eyes, really. Remo is feeding off the hints his eyes are giving. Remo presses down the gas. "Can't be easy with a brother like J. Slim. Big. Bad. Mean as shit. The money. All the power. All the pussy." Remo looks to the door. "That why you come here so much? You take the few dollars J. Slim gives you and you come here to feel better. Scraps to raise self-esteem. Here they have to respect you, right? It's part of the deal. What you pay a cover charge for."

Duffy looks away. Hollis thinks of slapping him again, but sees that Remo is working him over harder than Hollis ever could.

"What if I offer you a cut of what we take?" Remo nods as Duffy looks his way. "That's it. What if I give you a nice slice for yourself? A little something to go off and do your own thing. Start something new."

Duffy's eyes lock with Remo's. Ding. Ding. Remo has his hooks in deep.

"You'd do that?" Duffy asks.

"Just give me something good and I'm open to all kinds of shit."

"How good?"

"Start talking and I'll let you know when we get to something."

Duffy sticks his tongue in the side of his cheek. Eyes look to the ceiling. Remo knows the first thing Duffy gives him is going to be complete shit. He hopes Hollis is ready to slap the shit out of him when Duffy comes back with whatever weak-ass offer is coming.

"I got one," Duffy says, snapping his fingers. "There's the game he runs on—"

Remo snaps his fingers too.

Hollis slaps the shit out of Duffy. Sends him spinning to the floor again.

"Okay. Okay. Fuck me." Duffy looks for Remo to help him up again.

Remo does not. Remo simply stares back, waiting. Hollis crosses his arms.

"There's a big one," Duffy says. "Tomorrow morning. At an airport."

"Where?" Hollis asks, moving closer.

Duffy cowers. "White Plains, man. Tiny, private airport. Hangar with a strip of land. J. Slim is working an exchange—real dollars for funny money."

Remo looks to Hollis. They know the implication of this. They both know Ray has been working the counterfeit game hard for a while. If they can take this down it'll be US cash and God knows how much fake foreign currencies. This might work.

Could be huge.

Could be enough to move the needle.

Could be enough to make this right and get Anna and Sean out of harm's way.

Remo helps Duffy up and sits him down, flashing kind eyes as he says, "That's a good one, Duffy. We can work you a nice cut off that one."

"You better."

"Now, let's not go that way now. We were doing so well," Remo says, looking to Hollis.

Duffy recoils.

"You got a time?" Remo asks.

"I do."

"And you're sure about this thing?" Hollis says. "If you have us stepping into a shitstorm I will personally gut your weak bitch ass."

"No. It's real. It's huge. So huge..." Duffy trails off.

"What?" Remo asks.

"Might need more people."

Remo and Hollis share a look.

"What do you mean?" Remo asks.

"I mean this is a big fucking deal. There's going to be numbers, guns and muscle. You've got, what? How many of you? I'm a lover not a fighter. There's money to harvest, bro, I swear, but you're walking into a heavily armed situation."

Hollis starts to pace.

"How many of them?" Remo asks.

"Hard to say."

"Fucking guess."

"Ten, twenty."

"Thirty?" Hollis steps up. "Forty? Fifty?"

"It's possible," Duffy says. "Can I get a drink, too?"

"No," Remo says. "How much money?"

"Millions."

"Millions? Millions of real or millions of fake?" Remo asks.

"Both. Shit, man."

Hollis takes Remo aside. He talks clearly and deliberately, making sure each word lands with Remo. "I'm not saying no. You know I'm in, but if this fuckstick is telling the truth, this is one of those things that could start a war."

Remo nods. He knows, but he knows he doesn't have a choice.

"He's not wrong," Hollis says. "We need more people."

Remo turns to Duffy. "You got somebody in mind, don't you? Somebody to bring in."

Duffy grins and nods.

Remo and Hollis do not like the look he's giving.

"Well, who?" Remo asks.

"The Turkovs," Duffy says. "They reached out too. Just yesterday, but they just threatened to kill me. No money like you fine folks. I was actually here with Destiney as a little 'goodbye to the world' party."

"You know these Turkovs?" Remo asks Hollis. Hollis shakes his head no.

"Oh, you'll love them." Duffy laughs. "And they will sure as shit love you."

EVERYBODY'S COOL UNTIL THEY'RE NOT

Part II

CHAPTER EIGHT

Luxury by the square foot.

Windows stretch from the polished concrete floors to the ceiling giving a stunning view out onto the Hudson. Remo, Lester and Hollis stand a few feet behind Duffy. Duffy hasn't introduced everyone yet. He only stands, shakes and stares. Actually, he hasn't even spoken yet.

There's a dull thump as a body hits the floor across the room.

They pretend not to notice, but they do.

At a long table sit two Russian kingpins. The before-mentioned Turkovs. Not twins, but close. Big, all business, stone-cold killers. Turkov Brother One sets down his smoking .45, returning to his massive meal while seated next to his brother. Steaming plates of motherland goodness are laid out in front of them. Cabbage rolls, borscht and some shashlik are being destroyed by Turkov Brothers One and Two. Near the table are two well-dressed Russian thugs who try to hide their profession with expensive suits.

A cell buzzes by the borscht. Turkov Brother Two answers. "Yes?"

Remo, Hollis and Lester watch on as the gunshot-riddled body is dragged off by two more thugs using chains while the Turkov phone conversation continues.

"Yes," Brother Two says. "Then correct the problem. You've been a good friend and it is appreciated, but you cannot argue there have been bumps."

Brother One keeps working the food on his plate, stopping only to add, "Fuckin' bumps."

"Be sure your operation works better than your last stray little doggie we just took care of."

"Fuckin' doggie."

A chainsaw starts up in the background. Brother Two ends his call and stabs a chunk of beef with his fork. The brothers don't even pause their chewing as the chainsaw wails going to work in the other room.

To nobody in particular, Brother One says, "Fear and greed are only what moves people. This is why we have plenty of guns and money."

The brothers lock eyes with their guests. Making a point as the noise from the other room changes slightly. It's clear now the sound of the chainsaw has shifted to cutting flesh. The brothers return to their meal. Remo fights not to show his fear. Hollis and Lester are very skilled at either not being afraid at all or masking the hell out of it. Duffy is seconds away from pissing all over himself.

"You," Brother One says, motioning to Duffy. "The fuck you want? You bring friends this time. Why?"

Duffy clears his throat. Stops. Then starts again. He gives the Turkovs a quick, but more or less accurate, explanation of why Remo and company are there. Tells them that they want what the Turkovs want. They want to take down Ray and his White Plains airport operation. He explains who Remo is and how, maybe, they could help.

The chainsaw sound stops.

The Turkovs glance to one another.

"You," Brother One says to Remo. "Step up here."

Remo reluctantly moves up beside Duffy, tries a fake smile.

"Don't do that," Brother One says. "The smile, it's false, fuck that."

Remo's face drops.

"You a lawyer?"

Remo nods.

"I have no use for lawyers. You see we take care of things before there is a need for lawyer."

Brother Two raises his gun and puts two bullets into Duffy's chest.

Duffy spins then drops to the floor.

Remo jumps about a foot and a half. Lester and Hollis don't even blink. The two Russian thugs from before come back to the room with the chains and drag off Duffy's body. Remo's pretty sure he saw one of them roll their eyes, annoyed with the heavy workload.

"You see?" Brother One says. "No need for lawyer. Duffy was a cunt."

"Cunt," Brother Two says, returning to his meal.

"Mr. Turkov, both of you, we can help you," Remo says.

"Explain how you can help," Brother One says.

"We have guns. A lot of them. Clean. All of them. We have no use for them. We will give them to you as a gift." Remo gets nothing from them but dead eyes. "We also have this." He motions for Lester, who steps forward and sets down an envelope of cash. Cash they lifted from the Mashburn compound. Brother Two picks it up, thumbing through the bills.

Remo continues. "Not to mention you get the three of us on the job. Now think about it. That's guns, money and three hitters to help make this a smoother score."

Brother One leans back.

The chainsaw starts up again in the other room.

"Why?" he asks.

"Why what?" Remo asks back.

"Why do you want this so bad? Why so generous, or so desperate?"

"I need J. Slim."

The brothers perk up.

"You can have the take. The US dollars and the foreign funny money. I don't care about it. I need J. Slim alive. That's it. Period."

"Again, why?"

"He has my ex-wife."

"So?"

Remo pauses, thinks of laying on some serious bullshit but thinks better of it. He remembers his moment of honesty with Hollis and Lester. It worked. Worked like a charm. Given that Hollis and Lester probably share some of the same characteristics as these Turkov brothers, Remo thinks a similar tactic might work.

Can't hurt.

He hopes.

He takes a deep breath, swims through the bullshit he had loaded up, then looks deep, digging out the truth.

"And my son."

This stops the Turkovs cold. Their stares harden.

"J. Slim and Ray took my son."

There's a sudden, silent anger that seems to tighten their once blank faces. Remo has no idea what the genesis is, but there is an unmistakable shift in attitude. Maybe they have sons. Maybe they lost sons. Perhaps they are about to have sons or any combination thereof, but the second the word *son* left Remo's lips the mood changed.

The brothers nod together.

Remo looks back to Hollis and Lester. They know the same thing. These mean-ass Russians? They're all in.

Brother One says, "The enemy of my enemy is my friend."

Remo nods. *Indeed.*

The meaty hum of a chainsaw hitting flesh sounds from the next room.

Perhaps Destiny will remember Duffy fondly.

CHAPTER NINE

Oleg and Poe are two walls of Russian muscle, and they do not speak much.

Hardly at all.

These are the two men the Turkovs assigned/gave to them for assistance. They are big, intimidating and, from what they're told, deadly as hell. Remo unloaded the guns they took off the Mashburn compound along with a healthy sum of cash, as promised. The Turkovs grunted thanks of some sort and offered up these two muscle-bound, trigger-happy Russian death machines.

These fine boys, along with Remo, Lester and Hollis, are in the Yukon and headed to the place Duffy spoke of in White Plains. Hollis drives with Lester riding shotgun, and Remo sits sandwiched between Oleg and Poe in the back. The Turkovs wanted it this way so their people could keep an eye on things, and if something went the wrong way Oleg and Poe could gun down everyone in the car.

Forward-thinking, those Turkovs.

Remo can appreciate that.

Thankfully, Duffy gave the Turkovs all the info about the drop before they shot him in the chest and carved him up into cuts of beef. Truly a rookie move on Duffy's part. Never give up everything before the job. Never tell them that you've told them ALL they need to know. Always leave something, a piece of info, in your back pocket so they don't do to you exactly what they did to Duffy. Sad, but stupid doesn't last long in this business of sin, or any business for that matter, regardless of morality.

There's a small airport near White Plains, New York, with a warehouse or hangar or whatever you want to call it just off the runway. According to the Turkovs it's a private deal. So private and exclusive that only a handful of assholes know about its existence. It's as if a rectangle has been cut out of the trees, and then a tiny airport was dumped in.

The funny money drop is between some asshole criminals, not the Turkovs, and Ray's people. The Turkovs hate everyone involved and would really like it if Remo and company kill everybody there, but they are realistic. They'll settle for the cash, both funny and real, and as many deaths as humanly possible. They are not greedy people.

Remo isn't completely comfortable with the slaughter aspect of the Turkovs' plans, but he'll leave that up to Oleg and Poe. His focus is zeroed in on J. Slim. Remo, Lester and Hollis all know they are to grab him and get him to give up where Sean and Anna are.

That's it.

Simple.

Not easy, but not complicated either.

They may have to become, more or less, bodyguards for J. Slim once the party gets started. Once the bullets start popping and the shells start dropping things can get weird in a hurry. Nobody knows this more than Remo, Lester and Hollis. If J. Slim catches a stray 9mm to the skull, then this whole thing was a waste of time. Once they get to J. Slim they have to go full-on Secret

Service and protect him as if the free world depended on him. If J. Slim gets popped, then Anna and Sean are as good as dead.

Even the idea of that twists at Remo's guts. The idea he'd be the cause of that would be the end of Remo. That's it. If that's how this thing plays out, Remo will turn the gun on himself and lullaby his own ass. He's already decided it. Maybe it's the coward's way out, but Remo isn't all that concerned about his legacy at this point.

"Fuck that shit," Remo says to himself.

That isn't going to happen.

He's not a *power of positive thinking* type of dude, but he knows he can't allow the idea of failure to creep into his thinking. If you start thinking that way there's a possibility of you thinking scared. Scared makes you cautious. Makes you second-guess. Makes you waste time with thought and analysis. That fraction of a second you spend on that bullshit might be the difference between success and failure.

Or life and death.

Remo has to already think—sorry, *know*—in his heart that this battle is won and he's done what he had to do. In Remo's mind, the war has already been won. Anna and Sean are safe and everything is okay. Now all he has to do is paint by numbers and get this little exercise done. Lester and Hollis know what to do. Not a concern there. Oleg and Poe look like they've done this sort of thing before and have enjoyed it. Well, as much as they can enjoy anything.

Yeah, Remo and this crew, they're gonna make this shit look easy.

There's no way in hell they're going to storm that airport hangar, get mowed down in seconds flat by a wave of lead. No way Ray's psycho boy in NYC will kill Anna and Sean with a grin on his face.

That can't happen.

Not even possible.

No.

The hell with that shit.

Remo swallows big as the airport appears beyond the trees.

CHAPTER TEN

A plane cuts through the purple dawn sky.

Remo spots it in the distance, pointing it out to everyone in car as if he were a child seeing a plane for the first time. He's actually bouncing in his seat. The anxiety is getting to him. It's tearing, pulling at him, but he knows he can't let it rip him completely apart. He's been cool up until now, somewhat cool, but the weight of it all is starting to take its toll, and it shows. He's starting to exhibit some cracks. Frayed edges can no longer be hidden by ego and bravado. Lester and Hollis share a look between them, knowing they need to keep an eye on Remo. They are fairly sure he'll pull it together. They've known him to be a gamer recently, but you never know someone's breaking point until it snaps in two.

Everybody's cool until they're not.

Hollis parks the Yukon a safe distance from the airport, but close enough to get a good view of the comings and goings of the place. Lester and Oleg watch through high-powered binoculars. As the plane gets closer and closer to touchdown, they notice something else moving toward the airport. On the ground this time. There are two silver Cadillacs passing through the gates and pulling up to the metal hangar near the runway. Everyone in the car stops. Collective breath held. This is the moment they get some idea of how many people and what kind of firepower they are up against. They all know it.

Four armed goons step out from the Caddies. Armed, but not ridiculous.

"Now we got something," Lester says.

A grunt from Oleg. A collective sigh. They all lock eyes on the runway.

"Where's J. Slim?" Remo asks, his nervous energy lumping up into this throat.

"Don't see 'em yet," Lester says.

"Where the hell is he?"

"Just said I don't see him."

Oleg grunts. So does Poe.

"That's not okay," Remo says.

"What would you like him to do about it?" Hollis chimes in, trying to bring Remo back down to earth. "Dial it down, man."

"I'd like him to tell me that J. Slim is there. I'd love for him to tell me that piece of shit is there, because if he's not then this whole thing is one big motherfucking—"

"Got 'em," Lester says.

Remo turns quickly. Eyes wide. Like a dog that heard a cheese wrapper. He shoves Oleg to the side and plants his face against the glass to get a better view. They all watch J. Slim slip out from the back seat of the last Caddy. He's dressed to the nines, as usual, with his smug confidence front and center, even from this distance. J. Slim nods to his goons. From the trunks, large forty-pound black bags are unloaded, one after the other. The goons snatch them up, loading them into the hangar without a hint of ceremony, all under the watchful eye of J. Slim.

Remo's stare goes in and out of focus, only allowing his eyes leave J. Slim long enough to look to Hollis. They share the briefest of moments. Recognition. A memory shared between them. A memory of J. Slim. A story they both know.

The J. Slim story.

It's a rare thing when someone gets over on Remo and Hollis, but J. Slim is a rare bird indeed.

J. Slim was on a job. On a hit in Singapore.

Hollis was on a job. On a hit in Singapore.

They were both paid handsomely to eliminate a target by two separate parties. One had paid J. Slim and the other paid Hollis. An overlap in killer coverage. Not unheard of, but it doesn't happen very often.

Both of the killers were clients of Remo Cobb, so Remo being Remo, brokered a deal between Hollis and J. Slim that would allow them both to get credit for the kill and get them both paid by their separate parties. Their employers wouldn't care one way or the other. They cared about getting a corpse in return. Dead is dead no matter who does the deed. The idea being that two trained killers working together would almost guarantee a desired result without headaches. That is really what these people wanted in the end. It's not about the money, necessarily, it's about getting this dude done dead without problems. Problems can turn out to be more expensive than hitmen.

Of course, this all went to hell.

J. Slim and Hollis meticulously worked out the details. Combed over every single nuance. Went over the schematics of buildings. Street maps. Layouts of rooms. Weather patterns. They kept spreadsheets of comings and goings. They knew when his kids went to school, when his wife went to work and when he walked the dog. This was designed to be a clean, tight kill. One target. One body. No muss and certainly no fuss.

On the day of the thing J. Slim went in early.

Alone.

He went in without telling Hollis or Remo.

J. Slim went in and murdered everyone in the house. The

target, the wife, the kids and the dog. J. Slim said later it was to send a message. A clear message to others that would think about talking to the Feds as the target did.

Hollis beat the shit out of him.

Remo watched. Remo enjoyed watching, because he hated J. Slim just as much as Hollis for what he had done. Their shared hate had nothing to do with the job or the money. Like stated before, both paying parties just wanted the thing done, and then J. Slim went off on his own. He ignored the plan that was tight and clean and humane and didn't involve killing an innocent family. J. Slim did the job via a gas leak and a lit match while they were sleeping.

"No muss. No fuss," said J. Slim

Not how Hollis took it as he beat on J. Slim's face like he was tenderizing a roast. Remo held Hollis' gun and stood back, but was very supportive from the sidelines.

After taking a considerable pounding, J. Slim pulled his emergency blade from his ankle. Gave it a whip-slice. Cut Hollis across the chest, leaving a scar that Hollis still holds. This gave J. Slim enough of a break to escape. He slipped off back to Ray, never to been seen again. That was until J. Slim showed up at a CIA safe house in New Mexico not long ago.

Much to Remo's disgust.

Men like Hollis and Remo have learned to compartmentalize their hate and horror. It's the only way to survive their lines of work. The only way to deal with the ups and downs and the horrific humans they run across. Remo's compartmentalization has sprung some leaks as of late, but he had indeed put his box of J. Slim loathing aside until recently. Seeing him come out of the car in New Mexico opened it up however. Remo can't speak for Hollis, but he would like nothing more than to see a lot of blood loss from J. Slim.

No, Remo is pretty sure he can speak for Hollis on this one.

J. Slim face down in a puddle of his own blood would be agreeable.

That? That they can both get onboard with.

Remo stares out the window, watching J. Slim. Back to the here and now. His mind rolling, racing, ripping through the events that have passed and the moments that are passing before his eyes now. He checks the back. The Yukon is filled with guns.

Tools, Hollis calls them.

Indeed. Work needs to be done.

A lot of people are going to die. Remo is way past the morality of all that. A few days ago death bothered him. Gave him a moment of pause. A few days ago he didn't know what it was like to have your life truly in danger.

Now?

Now having his life on the line is his steady state. A constant, daily activity much like water, air and Johnnie Blue. Actually, now, meaning today, it's worse than that. Remo didn't think it could get worse, but he was wrong. Now, today, his family's lives are on the line, and that is not something Remo will ever get comfortable with. Yes, it's a strained family at best, but it is the only family he knows, and they don't deserve to be in the middle of this jacked-up, Remo-induced shitshow.

He snaps away from the path his brain has taken him on and turns his focus on the task at hand—the runaway, the hangar and the assholes with the Caddies. The bags have been removed and moved into the hangar. One can assume those bags are filled with money of some sort. Who knows how much green is in there? Who knows how much firepower waits in there? Who knows who or what is in that plane?

Hollis looks to Remo, then Lester. The three nod. This is what they do. Friends forged by chaos. Partners who've weathered some choppy-ass seas. Partners in their new, thrown-together startup—Mayhem Inc.

Oleg and Poe grunt while loading up 9mm sidearms, shotguns,

assault rifles and strapping on Kevlar vests. Lester and Hollis do the same. Oleg shoves a vest into Remo's chest.

He takes a deep breath.

The plane's wheels touch ground.

Shit just got real, real fast.

CHAPTER ELEVEN

The nondescript warehouse-looking plane hangar sits among several other run-down storage facilities.

Remo and the rest of Mayhem Inc. are now on foot. They stay slow and low, stopping frequently so they can study the target ahead and pivot to any changes that might pop up.

Like bullets and carnage.

The surrounding trees provide a good amount of cover for them to move in and out, along with some shade from a clear line of sight from the runway. Remo thinks they've come a long way from New Mexico to be right back in the woods about to storm into certain death. This seems to be new for Oleg and Poe. Hiking is not part of their skillset. They lean against trees catching their breath, but remain pissed-off looking and focused on the runway ahead.

Two of J. Slim's goons stand by the doors of the hangar. Watchful faces darting left and right. Suits, shades and guns. They roll the large steel doors open, allowing J. Slim and the rest of the goons to enter. At a quick count, there seems to be four, not counting J. Slim. All with hard looks and armed as hell. Five on five, Remo thinks, maybe another couple on the plane. Element of surprise riding on their side. This they can do without breaking a sweat.

Another Caddy pulls up. Five more armed goons step out.

"Fuck," Remo mutters.

J. Slim motions for his new friends to take positions. He stops just short of entering the hangar as he steals a peek at the plane that's now taxiing in.

Remo's not an expert on aircraft, but he thinks the plane is a Gulfstream G-something. He's flown in a couple of similar-looking jets before. Last-minute trips to Vegas, Aspen, Thailand and every place in between. All with clients. All with criminals, murderers and thieves. Remo guesses that's exactly what's about to stroll out of this Gulfstream G-something, too.

J. Slim waves to the plane as the door opens. He motions for his goons to make a move. A pack of them race over from the side of the hangar towards the plane as it rolls to a stop. The goons position themselves perfectly in line with the opening door of the plane as the stairs begin folding down. A few moments pass. Remo can see J. Slim smiling, but keeping a hand on his gun. Business-friendly without an ounce of trust.

From out of the plane steps what looks to be some muscle from that side of the deal. Eurotrash with a good tailor. All with five o'clock stubble, dark hair, dark complexions and dark, dark souls. Two of them carefully work their way down the stairs with assault rifles held tightly to their chests. They move with purpose, but don't rush, scanning the area while working their way down the stairs toward the hangar. One stays near the doors of the hangar in sight of the plane while the other goes inside.

Remo watches carefully to try and pick up anything they might give him. Some kind of info he can glean from appearances. From their faces. Their eyes.

Nothing.

Expressions? Stone-faced.

Talking? None.

Anything useful? Nope.

After a minute or so one of the Eurotrash muscle boys comes out from the hangar and gives a thumbs-up to the plane. Remo and the rest of his team share eyes, re-grip their guns, then move forward a few feet. They are still about fifty yards from the hangar, but close enough for striking distance.

They stop again, taking a new position behind some trees closer to the hangar. Out from the plane step two more walking slabs of Eurotrash muscle, followed by a three-hundred-pound man in a white suit, black tie, and a Yankees cap, puffing a cigarette like a chimney. Behind him is another batch of muscle. Remo has given up counting the goons and Eurotrash. It's doing more harm to his confidence than good.

"You know him?" Remo whispers to Oleg and Poe.

They shake their heads.

"Never seen Mr. Three Bills around before?" he asks again.

They look annoyed, but still shake their heads.

"You?" Remo asks, looking to Hollis and Lester. "You know Three Bills over there?"

Hollis and Lester both answer the same as Oleg and Poe.

Remo looks hard, trying to place him, but cannot. More than a little odd that no one from this group recognizes this guy. This is a group of people who know more than a few criminals. It's a big country, but a fairly small community, and word gets around. Especially ones who have big money. Three Bills appears to be connected to something. Something big. At least connected to Ray in some way.

Three Bills stops by the stairs and returns J. Slim's wave. He waits as two of his guys come from the back of the plane wheeling out two large silver cases about the size of coffins. Three Bills points them to the hangar. J. Slim watches as the cases are pushed past him and into the hangar. He pats the top of one. It takes a minute or two, but Three Bills eventually reaches J. Slim. They shake hands and enter the hangar together.

Once they are inside, the two goons stationed at the doors roll them shut with a loud, echoing clang. The goons get back into position, waiting outside the doors. Lester points out another two, who are walking around the outside of the hangar, and two Eurotrash muscle boys waiting by the plane.

Remo brings everyone in close. He speaks low, choosing his words carefully, because he knows he doesn't have much time to work with.

"You can murder every motherfucker in there. Do whatever you have to do, but J. Slim lives. Secure him, slap him around, whatever, but I need him with a functioning brain and the ability to speak. Got it?"

He looks around his team, making strong eye contact with each of them. Making sure he's heard loud and clear. There's a long pause, then he gets the response he wants. The nods come in one by one.

"Good. Now, let's see if we can do this without getting our asses shot to hell."

CHAPTER TWELVE

A whisper-zip of a bullet slices through the air.

A goon's head explodes.

The body drops.

Another whisper-zip.

A second goon's head explodes. That body drops.

Hollis has fired two bullets, dropped two goons and cleared the entrance for him and his team without a single extra beat of his heart.

Calm.

Cool.

Precise murder.

This is what Hollis does. Lester, Oleg and Poe move fast out from the trees. They hit the Eurotrash muscle hard, moving like lightning. They work their knives to slice the life away from them.

Quiet.

Only the wind.

Airplane is now cleared. Remo stands next to Hollis by a tree just off the runway. Hollis's breathing is slow and steady, tracking the area through his scope. Remo fights his breathing that desperately wants to go apeshit. He works hard, keeping it under wraps, but he has to gasp, wheeze and cry. Hollis waits patiently. He wants the other two goons to round the hangar so he can remove them from the planet just as he did the two by the hangar doors. Lester, Oleg and Poe take cover behind one of the Caddies, checking their weapons. Waiting for Hollis to drop these clowns.

Seconds crawl. Creep. Each one more painful than the next.

Seems like hours.

Unbearable.

The first one comes around the corner, stops and lights a cigarette. The two dead goons with freshly popped skulls are close by, lying not far from his feet. Hollis knows he needs to get a visual on both of them before he can fire. Does him no good to drop one and then have the other go berserk and start yelling, shooting or making phone calls for reinforcements.

Lester sees the other goon. One Hollis and Remo can't see from where they are.

The goon's texting near the back corner of the hangar. The goon with the cigarette is now only a few feet from stumbling over the dead bodies. If he finds them and goes berserk, then this thing gets set off and shit gets much, much more complicated.

Hollis knows it.

Remo knows it.

Everybody knows it.

Remo looks to Lester. Lester can't maneuver to get anywhere near Texting Goon without the other one spotting him. Lester points toward the back corner, letting Remo and Hollis know where Texting Goon is located. Cigarette Goon takes a step forward without looking, his toe barely an inch or two away from the body on the ground.

Remo can feel this whole thing going to hell. In his mind, he can envision everything falling apart and drifting away. The mistakes that can happen when panic and fear set in. The coveted element of surprise can go to shit in a hurry when everyone is armed, dangerous and scared as hell. Bullets fly. People you don't want dead end up dead. Remo can see J. Slim catching a bullet and getting killed before Remo can find out where Anna and Sean are.

He can't let that happen.

That will not happen.

He checks his Glock, thinks, then grabs the Sig Live Free or Die knife off of Hollis's ankle. Hollis looks at him like *what the hell are you doing?* Remo runs hard around the other side of the hangar, away from Cigarette Goon, with his gun in one hand and the knife in the other. Lester and Hollis look to one another with arms out. *What the hell is he doing?*

Hollis returns his focus back on Cigarette Goon. It's a delicate game here. If that goon can clear the corner and get out of sight from Texting Goon then Hollis can take him out. But he can't fire until Cigarette Goon is out of sight, and if Cigarette Goon moves too much farther he'll see the bodies for sure. Hollis tracks his face for two reasons. One, to pull the trigger and remove half of it. Two, to see if his expression changes to something that reads like *holy shit, dead bodies.*

Remo reaches the back of the hangar. He slows to a walk, doing his best to quiet his steps. He can hear a cough from around the corner. Maybe only a few feet from where Remo is standing.

Hollis keeps his finger on the trigger.

Remo inches closer and closer. He pulls the Sig knife back.

Cigarette Goon's toe touches a dead goon's body.

He stops, looks down, then looks up.

"Shit," Hollis whispers to himself.

Hollis drops Cigarette Goon with a zip-shot between the eyes.

Remo rounds the corner, finding Texting Goon, who's no longer texting. He's got his back to Remo looking toward the front of the hangar where his smoking buddy's body just leaned back, straightened, swayed, then slumped to the ground.

"Fuck," Remo says.

It happened so fast.

He can't believe he said it out loud.

He simply let the word slip from his mouth. Texting Goon spins back around to Remo. Remo lunges hard, slamming his hand over the goon's mouth. The second he does it he realizes he should have done something different. Hollis would have just slashed the guy's throat without thinking about it. Lester would have destroyed him before he could have turned around in the first place. This is the difference between Remo and them. Crazy and sane. Killer and not. Remo is tougher and stronger than he was a few days ago, but he is not a natural born killer, and if he's being honest, he doesn't want to be.

Remo manages to cover the goon's mouth, forcing him down to the ground. He slaps his cell phone away as it buzzes with a new text. The goon throws a punch, tagging Remo in the nose. A muted crunch. Remo falls back a bit giving the goon a second of freedom. The goon flips over, reverse crab-crawling away. Remo leaps forward, landing on the goon's back and jamming an elbow in his back and a hand under his chin forcing his mouth closed. Remo whips and rocks. Rough-riding him like a mechanical bull cranked to intense. He holds on for dear life, makes it maybe two seconds.

A whisper-zip.

Remo hits the ground face-first. Skids.

The body that was throwing him like a rag doll went completely limp. In a snap. Just like that. Looking up from the dirt, Remo sees Hollis and Lester standing at the other end of the hangar.

Hollis lowers his rifle. Lester gives a thumbs-up. Oleg and Poe stare.

"Fuck," Remo says again. His face throbs. He can feel the blood dripping from his nose. Hopes the dirt will slow the flow.

Lester helps Remo to his feet, handing him his gear. They

each pull down classic bank robber ski masks and walk toward the entrance of the hangar. No discussion. The plan is still a green light. They decided that covering their faces was the best way to go. No reason to advertise who they are on the off chance that anyone comes out of this party alive.

Remo and Mayhem Inc. ready themselves at the doors.

Lester carefully places his hands on the door's handle, ready to slide it open on command. Remo's command. Hollis has slung the rifle over his back and positioned an AR ready to go. Oleg and Poe check their sidearms and ankle knives. Remo gives Hollis his Sig back. The Russians set their ARs as well. Remo, not Hollis's suggestion, will stick with the Glock 9mm. Hollis wanted Remo to go in heavy just like everybody else. Even though Remo had used some heavy tools during the Mashburn ambush at his place in the Hamptons, Remo is more comfortable with the handgun. Not sure why. Feels right.

Remo stands with Hollis on one side with Poe and Oleg behind them and Lester at the door. Hollis went over some sweeping techniques earlier and he hopes to hell that information sunk into these thick, dickhead skulls. He kept it basic, but ya know, it's all about the audience.

Taking a moment of pause, Remo stops to reset. A second to breathe. He hasn't done much of it in the last few minutes. Perhaps it's a mistake to stand here and think about what he's about to do. About what he's about to walk into. All the potential violence that's waiting beyond that door. The amount that will be inflicted on both sides. The blood that will spill and splat. The screams of pain and the ending of life.

Perhaps Remo's got it all wrong.

Perhaps it will go peacefully. Remo can get J. Slim and Oleg and Poe can grab their money and then Remo will find Anna and Sean and everything will be fine. Just fine. Remo knows that's absolute bullshit, but he finds the idea comforting. At least at a time like this. Power of positive thinking. Glass half full and all that.

Hollis looks to the frozen Remo.

Hollis spanks him on the ass. Hard.

Remo snaps back to the here and now.

He smiles, then nods to Lester to open death's damn door.

CHAPTER THIRTEEN

The hangar is empty save for a few long tables with a few more goons stationed at each table.

Next to them are clipboards, paperwork and heavy-duty money counting machines. Bags are systematically emptied on the tables. Goons and Eurotrash take their places watching over as the others pull out stacks and stacks of fresh, shrink-wrapped cash. The goons count and check the contents of the bags under the watchful eyes of J. Slim and Three Bills. Their focus is hard, but they try to hang onto a level of cool. At least J. Slim does. Three Bills gave up on cool a long time ago.

The hangar is silent save for the rhythmic flipping of bills running through counting machines. No one speaks. Moderate eye contact.

Three Bills busts up the quiet by leaning over to J. Slim and saying, "If there's a penny missing, I'm cutting off balls."

J. Slim nods, acknowledging the threat but not necessarily concerned by it. The room goes back to the white noise soundtrack of money counting.

The door gives a clang, then a rattling shudder.

All heads whip around at the same time.

Pause.

Another clang with a shudder of metal. The door shakes harder and harder.

It's stuck.

There's a muffled sound of, "Motherfucker!"

Pause.

The sound of a fist banging on the door from the outside.

Three Bills looks to J. Slim. *You expecting someone?*

He shrugs, then motions to his goons to check the door. All eyes on the front doors with hands on guns and fingers on triggers. The goons pull the doors open, revealing a masked squad. A masked Remo squad armed with enough firepower to take over a small country.

ARs get planted on the goons' heads before they can get off a single shot. The remaining members of the masked crew pour in with military precision. Guns tracking on the goons, Eurotrash, J. Slim and Three Bills.

"Don't move, motherfuckers!" a masked Hollis barks. His voice booms and echoes in the open space.

Remo's the last one through the door. Shoves a goon inside the hangar to the floor, then slides the door shut. Not all the way —doesn't want that embarrassing stuck shit to happen again—but enough to hide a clear view inside. He turns his attention to J. Slim, making sure of where he is at all times.

Poe removes the barrel from one goon's head then cracks his jaw with the butt of his AR, putting him to the floor with a bounce. He zip-ties two goons and removes their guns, sliding them across the floor toward the corner of the hangar.

Remo can't help but be impressed.

Those Russian dudes don't talk much, but they can work a room like a bad bunch of bastards. He'll be sure to let the Turkovs know. Maybe it'll show up on their review.

Hollis works the rest of the room. "Faces on the floor, palms flat." He looks to his watch timer ticking down. "Forty-two seconds."

"Fuck you," Three Bills spits out. "I will kill each and every one of you piece of shit mother—"

Hollis slams his AR into Three Bills's ample stomach then rips the butt up to his chin, leveling all three hundred pounds of him in a split second. The remaining goons and Eurotrash follow orders, going down quickly to the floor with hands flat on the concrete. Oleg and Poe move quickly, securing their hands with flex cuffs, all while removing guns, cells and emergency weapons from ankles. They move with absolute fluidity. Not a single motion wasted, every movement has purpose.

J. Slim still stands.

He burns as he watches these masked men pick up bag after bag. Remo steps over to him, standing a few inches from his face. J. Slim smiles. Remo thinks of blowing his head off. This is the second time in a matter of days he's considered shooting this guy. Once in New Mexico, and now in a secluded airstrip in White Plains, New York. No matter the locale, the desire to blow this fucker's brains out remains strong.

"You are so dead," J. Slim says. "You get me? All of you are ghosts, you just don't know it."

"Shut up, dildo," Remo says through grinding teeth.

J. Slim cocks his head. "Remo?" He smiles bigger now. "That you in there?"

"Fuck."

Remo cracks J. Slim upside the head with the butt of his gun. J. Slim's legs wilt underneath him. He slumps, then falls to the floor in a lump of asshole.

"Oh shit," Remo mutters.

He drops to his knees, trying to wake J. Slim up. In a moment of panic mixed with amped-up hostility he cracked J. Slim in the temple. He just knocked out the one guy he needs in this whole fucking thing. The one person he needs to be upright and speaking. The one who knows where Anna and Sean are located.

"Shit. Fuck. Shit," Remo stammers as he tries to open J. Slim's eyes with his gloved fingers. It's not working. He tries petting his hair. Tries talking sweetly. None of it's working. J. Slim is down. Out cold.

Lester comes over with a money bag thrown over his shoulder. He looks down. "That's not good."

"No shit," Remo says.

"What'd you do?"

"Nothing."

"Nothing?"

"I didn't do shit."

"He just fainted?"

Remo pauses. "Yes."

Lester nods, knowing that's complete bullshit, but lets it go. He bends down and cuffs J. Slim's hands and removes his weapons.

"Just in case he wakes up," he says, with a hint of patronizing.

Oleg and Poe dig through one bag and pull out the multiple shrink-wrapped bricks of various foreign currencies. All fake as hell, but impossible for the naked eye to catch. They both nod. Perhaps they're happy. Perhaps they know the Turkovs will be happy. Who can tell? The two slabs of Russian beef throw the bags over their shoulders. Hollis checks his watch, throwing the last bag over his shoulder. The entire takedown took less than ninety seconds.

Hollis smiles.

Still got it.

He twirls his finger in the air. Poe nods. It's the signal for him to run out and bring the Yukon around so they can load up the bags and get gone. Poe runs hard out the door like a well-trained Labrador.

"There's more cash on the plane," Three Bills says.

"What?" Hollis spins around with his AR pointed down at Three Bills's face.

"Two more bags," Three Bills says, looking up. "Close to two million. Some good going away money. My people will still hunt you down, can't stop that, but that two million out there? That'll help you buy some time. For a bit at least."

Hollis looks to Lester and Remo. Remo is still deeply concerned about the health of J. Slim. He's sitting with J. Slim's head in his lap, petting his hair gently.

"You let me back on that plane," Three Bills says, "and you can have all the money in there."

Lester and Hollis both know that no matter what happens, they need as much money as they can grab. Hollis turns to Oleg.

"Cut it up? Fifty-fifty?" Hollis asks.

Oleg nods, yanking at Three Bills's elbow, working to get him up to his feet.

"I need one of my guys," Three Bills says. "He's the only one who can fly the damn thing."

"Bullshit," Hollis says.

"It's true," Three Bills says, pointing to one of the Eurotrash boys on the floor. "Damn lucky you didn't kill him. He can fly us out. You've taken the guns off us. What's he gonna do?"

Hollis breathes out, then nods.

Lester goes over to Remo and helps him pick up J. Slim. They work his cuffs so they can throw his arms over their shoulders and let his feet drag between them. It's a pretzel of a move, but it's working. Oleg and Hollis move behind with guns tracking Three Bills and his pilot as they all exit the hangar.

Stepping out into the light of day.

Stepping over the dead goons on the ground, they move toward the plane with Three Bills and Eurotrash out front and Hollis and Oleg behind them. Lester and Remo wrestle with the dead weight of the passed-out J. Slim. He's a big guy and he's not helping. Remo hates himself. Hates how stupid he is. He just hopes he didn't catch J. Slim in the one spot of the head that'll turn him into a vegetable or slip into a coma or break his memory. Remo shakes his head, beating himself up on the inside.

Lester sees what Remo is doing to himself. "Not your fault."

"Oh, but it is."

"True, you did this, but this is a fluid fight and things happen. He's still breathing. We simply need to wait."

"You sure?"

Lester thinks for a moment. "No."

Poe pulls up fast in the Yukon. Lester and Remo load J. Slim into the back, along with bags of money and close the back hatch. They turn to watch the others walking toward the plane. Remo scans the area. He can't believe they've done it. They're going to make it. Sure, it's had some snags. Some hiccups here and there, and they still have a ways to go, but this leg of the thing is working.

He reflects on how he got here. Allows himself to take a moment of pride in the fact he's still alive and still has chance. Given the circumstances that's not bad. Many a man would have crawled under a table and cried. Remo smiles. *Who's the man?*

He grabs the iPad, taking the opportunity to check in on Anna and Sean.

There are some new images now. It's no longer the psycho watching and following his ex-wife and son. They are all in the same room now. The iPad has been set up in a dirty, beaten up, slum of a room. It's set up so it has a view of Anna and Sean seated on a filthy couch with the psycho seated next to them.

The psycho smiles and waves. Anna and Sean are scared. Something in Remo unhinges. He feels himself falling away. His helplessness has reached a new and unthinkable level. He grips the iPad hard, screaming into the screen. Lester grabs Remo by the shoulders, trying to control him. Hoping to comfort his friend. Veins in Remo's neck pop. His face rushes to red. He doesn't want to see, but he stares into the screen. They look unharmed, but frightened as hell.

Remo wants to kill these people. He wants to grind their bones and eat their souls. Lester grabs Remo by the face, speaking calmly and directly while looking into his eyes. "We'll get it done."

Remo shakes.

Lester repeats the words. Remo comes down slightly. He nods.

A crack sounds out from the distance. Lester and Remo whip around toward the plane and the group walking toward it.

The Eurotrash pilot's head explodes.

Remo's hand lets the iPad slip from his fingers. A momentary lapse of concentration sends his window to Anna and Sean falling down. The screen cracks upon impact with the runway's blacktop. Through the spiderweb of busted glass Remo sees Sean's terrified face before the screen goes black.

CHAPTER FOURTEEN

Gunfire erupts from every direction. Everyone freezes.

Except Remo.

Remo's sole focus is on the nonresponsive iPad. He's dropped to his knees, holding it as if it was a crying child.

Remo's tongue becomes fat, too big for his mouth. He fumbles around words, stuttering nonsense, only able to get out, "What's happening?" He says it over and over again. Remo is completely stunned, stuck, frozen by the chaos that's swelling up around him. He can't get his mind around the speed with which it happened. How quickly it's all come undone. The relentless, ferocious nature of the deteriorating situation has him floating in a void.

Lester shoves him into the Yukon as Hollis races toward them ducking, weaving, trying to avoid the firepower from an enemy unseen. Poe and Oleg dive in the back. Hollis hits the hood with full force, coming to a stop, spins off, then slides in behind the wheel. Bullets pop and rip. A shot tags the hood. Hollis punches the ignition, slams it in reverse and jams down the pedal. Tires scream as the Yukon flies backward toward the open gate behind them.

"What's happening?" Remo repeats, still clinging to the busted iPad.

Two black sedans move in fast through the gates, headed straight toward them at ramming speed. Unmarked cops or feds, hard to tell. Hollis locks up the breaks. The black sedans stop and men dressed in jeans and T-shirts covered by Kevlar vests pour out from the cars with guns raised and ready.

A stream of bullets knocks the Kevlar dudes down. Holes punch the front of the black sedans.

A driver takes a few in the face through the windshield.

Three Bills is racing toward the Yukon with a full-auto AR, firing wildly at what's left of the black sedans.

"Let me the fuck in," Three Bills yells, pointing his AR at the windshield. "Now, bitches."

More bullets zip from an unseen source.

More black sedans come screaming in from the other direction. Headed right at them. Lester flies out from the Yukon, blasting toward the sedans hauling ass toward them down the runway. He flings open the back door for Three Bills to get in. All three hundred pounds of him jumps in, landing in the laps of Oleg and Poe and on top of Remo, who hadn't had an opportunity to sit up yet.

"Son of bitch," Remo yelps, barely able to breathe, let alone speak.

"Get in the damn car," Hollis yells to Lester.

Lester rips a last stream of suppression fire then hops back in. Hollis turns the wheel hard, slams into D and punches it. Putting the pedal down, the Yukon whips around, pulling hard Gs, heading around the decimated black sedans and out the gate.

Bullets zip and whiz past the window as they pull away.

The black sedans clear the plane, speeding toward the Yukon. More vested men poke out from the windows, blasting away at the Yukon as they give chase.

"Get the fuck off me you fat motherfucker," Remo yells, struggling to get out from under. He wrestles and tugs himself free, gasping for air. The sudden loss of oxygen and fear of being buried alive has hit reset. Remo has put the iPad and the psycho on hold. "Who the hell is that out there?" Remo asks, spinning, looking out the back window, trying to get a look at the sedans running rip-shit after them.

J. Slim jolts up from the back, sitting straight up with his face firing up about an inch from Remo's nose.

Remo shrieks.

Slams the butt of his Glock against the side of J. Slim's head.

J. Slim slumps back down.

"Shit!" Remo yells.

Oleg and Poe wrestle Three Bills's gun away from his sausage fingers.

"Who was on you?" Remo yells at Three Bills.

"Hell if I know," Three Bills says. "Cops, feds ... they're always on us. Fuckin' popular."

The Yukon burns down the winding backcountry road with the sedans a few clicks behind. The engines roar. Tires fight for traction. Hollis's knuckles pop as his fists tighten on the wheel. Oleg and Poe lock and load. Lester, cool. Mad as hell, but cool. Three Bills a hostile mess.

Remo is about to shit himself.

His mind caves in.

Sensory overload crashing, overloading everything in his battle-weary brain. This is when he should consider giving up. They've reached the point when a sane person would let it all go. Simply accept that he gave it all a good try and realize that life wasn't meant to work out for people like him. Oh well, you play the hand you're dealt.

Remo knows that style of thinking won't work here. Not today.

There are other people involved who need him to pull his shit together and figure this all the fuck out. The last look he got at

Sean is burned into his brain. Remo can't allow that to be how he remembers his boy. Let that be the image he sees day after day. That will haunt him when he sleeps. When he wakes.

"Fuck that," Remo says. He dumps the clip from his Glock. He's not sure he even fired a shot during all this, but it seems like the thing to do. He jams in a fresh one.

Remo's eyes go wide, almost popping from his head.

Through the front windshield three new black sedans pull up ahead in the middle of the road. They park in a sideways position, blocking the road ahead. T-shirt and vest boys jump out, taking positions behind the cars.

Remo swallows hard.

Poe and Oleg don't even hesitate.

CHAPTER FIFTEEN

Poe and Oleg open up through the front windshield with rapid pops of fire.

Shells fling and bounce off the ceiling and leather of the Yukon. Jumping all around Remo and Three Bills. Hollis, with one hand on the wheel, follows Oleg and Poe's lead, blasting his Glock while slamming down on the gas. The Yukon jerks forward racing headlong toward the barricade like a runaway crazy train.

Up ahead in the middle of the road, the vest boys drop and roll like bowling pins. Some take bullets. Some dive clear. The Yukon plows between the sedans, ramming through, splitting two cars as it mows past. Front end smashed, bumper twisted, the Yukon skids, tilts on two wheels, then finally gains control, landing back down on all four tires, and keeps moving. Slowing down was never considered.

Gunfire from sedans behind them blows out the back window.

Oleg and Poe whip around in a single motion and continue their blasting back toward the enemy behind them. Remo looks back over the seat, checking on J. Slim. He's breathing, but covered in broken glass. Still out cold.

Through the blown-out window it looks like there are more of them now. More sedans have joined the party, also joined by state cruisers with reds blazing, pulsing along the tops of the cars in bars of lights.

Hollis drives like a madman. He reloads, blasting back at the cops and feds while driving with his free hand. Remo's eyes dance, brain clicking at the speed of light. Doesn't participate in the gunplay. His thoughts are torn apart, trying to formulate a plan on what the hell to do.

This was not discussed. This was not mapped out or diagrammed.

Tearing down the road, the Yukon rams headlong toward an entrance to a bridge. Hollis's eyes go wide. He doesn't want to get on that bridge. There's traffic up there. Not crazy, but enough to add to the complications they already have.

He tries to take a hard right to a side road—no dice.

Another black sedan slams into the side of them, forcing them straight ahead. The Yukon and sedan crash sides, ramming back and forth into one another as the Yukon passes any chance to stay off the bridge.

Poe fires into the sedan. The sedan peels off, slamming off the shoulder of the road and barely missing diving down into a ditch. The driver's dead. Head a limp, bloody mess. The remaining vest boy tries to steer from the passenger side, still slamming into the Yukon, coming off and on the road from the shoulder.

One more sedan pulls up alongside the driver's side of the Yukon. Now one on each side. Forcing them on the path onto the bridge. Poe and Oleg exchange fire with the sedans. One vest boy tries to shoot out the tires. Oleg leans out, putting a bullet into his face. Both the black sedans and Yukon ramble on. Bullets flying back and forth. Sounds popping. Steel tearing. All ramming at breakneck speed onto the bridge.

The New Croton Reservoir Bridge.

A steel, through arch bridge over New Croton Reservoir on Taconic State Parkway. It clocks in at seven hundred and fifty-foot-long steel suspended arch trusses with riveted structural steel members. The deck is a cast-in-place concrete deck with a concrete wearing surface. The approaches are enclosed chambers with solid beams. A stretch of steel and rock filled with innocent civilians rolling through their day. Traffic is moderate, but enough, and moves at a decent pace. Commuters, truckers, families all go about their days, completely unaware of what is coming up behind them.

The Yukon screams onto the bridge at high speed, weaving in and out of traffic as if it were standing still. Black sedans on their ass. New York State cruisers follow, though some peel off to block more traffic coming onto the bridge.

Gunfire between the Yukon and pursuers continues. Shells fall from windows, bouncing off the concrete. Innocent drivers lock up brakes and swerve out of the way. Smashing into one another, slamming into the guardrails and spinning to a stop.

The seeds of chaos taking root.

Cars and trucks filled with unsuspecting innocents peel off to the side as the war rages on. The Yukon is almost neck and neck with the cavalry of feds and cops behind them.

Poe and Oleg both fire with reckless abandon.

The feds and cops try to dodge the cascading walls of bullets being thrown down on them while firing back best they can, while trying not to kill civilians. Hollis keeps blasting. Cutting and jerking the wheel, trying to dodge the streaming panic that's sliding and braking along the bridge. The Yukon rams the back edge of the bumper on a Ford F-150. Everyone inside jerks forward then back hard as hell. Oleg sends an errant spray of lead into the air then pulls himself back down, blowing the windshield of a black sedan all to hell.

Screeching tires, crunching metal and the crack of gunfire is mind-numbing. Too much to bear. The F-150 the Yukon clipped begins to spin, locks up its brakes, causing the cars behind to slam into it.

Sparks off a chain reaction of traffic slamming into one another—a five-car pileup and growing by the second. In the wake of the Yukon and the F-150 is nothing but feds and cops. The innocent bystanders have either wrecked a couple hundred feet back or were lucky enough to find safety.

Hollis's eyes pop wide.

An 18-wheeler has jackknifed up ahead, creating a makeshift wall blocking the other end of the bridge. They're unable to see around it. No idea what's on the other side. The Yukon locks up the brakes, skidding to a stop just shy of the disaster ahead of them.

FBI and cops lock up to a tire-shredding stop about a hundred yards behind them.

Battle lines are being drawn.

The feds and cops on one side and Mayhem Inc. on the other, with an 18-wheeler providing a wall of sorts behind them. A pileup of innocent cars in the distance behind the line created by the feds and cops. Civilians bolt from the wreckage. Some bloodied, others only stunned or mildly injured. Several scurry to escape while clawing and climbing as far away as possible.

Oleg and Poe spring out from the Yukon. Guns locked and loaded. Ready for anything and everything. Eyes hard. Thoughts singular, focused, as spit flies from their lips and battle cries rage from their throats.

Remo slips out from the Yukon, trying to fight through the chemical impulses roaring through his veins. He scrambles behind the large SUV. Fear, confusion, fear. Thoughts of his family fly. Sean's face. Anna's looks. His eyes slam shut.

Hollis and Lester fall out, joining him. Watching the insanity of Oleg and Poe. The ruthless, reckless abandon they're operating under. Their bullets land only a few feet from innocent civilians simply trying to escape. Remo feels it in his chest—this isn't right. Not what he wants at all.

"They're out of control," Remo screams, pointing to Oleg and Poe.

Hollis nods.

"They can't carve up innocent people, goddammit. It's all fucked up."

Lester nods.

Remo peeks around the Yukon.

The feds and cops do their best to get out and take a position as bullets fly from the rampaging Oleg and Poe. Three Bills has joined them at the front of the Yukon, blasting away with his AR. A cop takes one in the shoulder. A fed pulls him behind a car, returning fire only to get spun around by another bullet.

Remo looks to the right of where he's crouched. One police cruiser and one unmarked black sedan are trapped in the middle, along with an ambulance, an RV and a Civic on fire. A dead driver slumps out the Civic's window. Flames roar from under the hood. A lone vest boy shot up in the driver side of the unmarked car.

A cop slips out from the car, dodging Oleg's and Poe's gunfire.

They load and unload without hesitation or a hint of compassion.

Remo pulls his Glock. Alternates his aim between Oleg, Poe and Three Bills. Has a perfect shot on them.

No idea what to do.

Take out these guys and end this now or hold back?

Opportunity burns away with every second. Mind fumbles for the right decision. Take the shot or not? He looks to Hollis. He isn't shooting at the cops either. Neither is Lester. This isn't what they signed up for.

Remo looks behind them at the 18-wheeler that has them walled off from the other side of the bridge. He thumbs behind him. "What if we jack another car and haul ass the hell the other way."

Hollis raises his eyebrows. *Maybe.*

Lester shrugs.

Remo ducks and weaves through the gunfire, making it to the edge of the front bumper of the jackknifed 18-wheeler. He can taste the way out of here. Another alternative to dying on a bridge filled full of holes and regret. Gunned down like a dog. As he peeks around the edge his hope dies a sudden, painful death.

The other side of the bridge is a line of police cruisers with red lights pulsing in and out. Cops with shotguns and handguns shielded by a wall of cars, leaning on hoods and trunks with their aim dead on them. They're waiting for the word. The word that'll cut them loose to come storming in.

But who's giving the word?

Remo spins back around the other side of the 18-wheeler. The opportunity he dreamt of is gone before it even started. Remo ducks down as a bullet screams by inches from his head. He ignores the near death.

His face is twisted. He's agonizing. *What the hell does he do now?*

He thinks. His mind on fire. There has to be something. He races back to Hollis and Lester behind the Yukon. They can tell by the look on Remo's face that the way out beyond the 18-wheeler is not a viable option.

The cops and vest boys are outgunned. The trio of madness made up of Oleg, Poe and Three Bills is terrifying, impressive in their ability to lay down wave after wave of punishing firepower.

Remo notices the shooting has almost completely stopped from the side of the bridge beyond the Yukon. He fights to get his bearings back. Steadies his fumbling mind. Looking around, he starts surveying the situation at lightning speed.

His thoughts slam into place.

Remo works his way toward Oleg, Poe and Three Bills, who've now moved up and taken cover behind an abandoned, shot-up Camry. His stomach drops fifty feet. A bad situation looks even worse up close. Oleg and Poe blast at the cops like men possessed. Loving it. Yelling out their disturbing war cry. Three Bills jiggles and bounces like a man made of marshmallow holding a jackhammer.

"Stop with the shooting, dammit," Remo yells at the three of them.

They continue blasting away.

"Hey. Assholes," he screams. "Stop firing your fucking guns."

Still nothing.

Remo, being a master of improv, does what he feels is the correct and only way to go in this particular situation. The only proven method he's seen over the years. He starts kicking these motherfuckers in the balls.

Starting with Three Bills, then Oleg and last Poe.

One after the other they fold.

The last shot fired by Poe leaves a faint echo in the air. The bridge goes eerily silent. Remo takes this moment of silence to seize an opportunity to get his message across.

"Sorry about the balls, but you were not listening." Remo talks while keeping an eye on the cops and what he now can safely guess are feds. "They will keep sending wave after wave at us until we're either out of bullets or dead. We have to work out a deal with these people."

"Fuck you," Three Bills says through gritted teeth.

Oleg and Poe stare hate-holes into him.

"We. Are. Trapped," Remo says. "I'm going to talk to them. It's the only way we're going to get out of this thing."

Oleg grabs Remo by the throat while shaking his head no.

"Dude. There's not another way," Remo says while gagging. "They've got us totally boxed in."

Hollis and Lester move up next to them while staying low. Remo looks to them, his friends, to help remove this big-ass Russian's hand away from his throat.

They do not. They understand Oleg's point of view.

"Look," Remo says. His speech is strained as his face gets

redder and redder. "Let me try at least. If it doesn't work you can always start shooting again."

Oleg lets his eyes slip over to Poe, looking for direction. An opinion from a co-worker. Poe thinks, then nods. Oleg releases Remo's throat, letting him fall back to the concrete of the bridge.

For a fraction of a second Remo gets a gorgeous view of the blue sky. Fluffy clouds roll by as if nothing's wrong. A bird soars by without a care in the world. For this brief sliver of time Remo has disconnected from his current disaster. Allowed himself to leave this place. A micro-vacation from hell. It's nice. He's glad the universe allowed him this moment.

He's rudely snapped out of it by the sound of someone yelling his name.

It's not anyone from his little group here.

Not Hollis or Lester or Three Bills, and certainly not Oleg or Poe.

Remo does, however, recognize the voice.

"Remo! Remo Cobb!" the voice yells again, louder this time.

Remo turns his head. He now realizes that when he fell back from Oleg's grasp he left his head out in the open in full view. Exposed. Free from the cover of the Camry and for all to see from the other side. Across the bridge he sees something. Someone he recognizes. Across the enemy lines is a lone familiar face.

A face Remo does not like.

"Remo!" Detective Harris screams across. He picks up a bullhorn and tries again. "Remo fucking Cobb!"

CHAPTER SIXTEEN

Last time Remo saw Detective Harris was in New York City.

Last time he saw this guy was when Detective Harris introduced Remo to CIA man Cormack in a bland interrogation room at a police station. Remo was there, or so Remo thought, to talk to Detective Harris about the events that took place at Remo's house in the Hamptons. The events that led to a few dead Mashburn brothers and damn near killed Remo. Remo had no idea what Detective Harris had in mind at the time. Not a clue that he wanted to introduce Cormack into Remo's life.

For those keeping score, CIA man Cormack has spent the last couple of days trying to get Remo and his friends killed. He sent them out on a couple of suicide missions and things eventually ended with Cormack dead, slumped over with half a head, but not before Cormack let the entire criminal underworld know Remo double-crossed the Mashburns. This information has led the criminal underworld to be all over Remo. The most notable is J. Slim, and this is the reason Remo's sitting in the middle of a war zone atop a bridge he can't get off of.

"Remo!" Detective Harris calls out again.

Simple math dictates that Detective Harris directly or indirectly, more than likely directly, tried to get Remo killed and put his ex-wife and son in great danger. Remo feels his blood pressure spike. His face runs hot.

He stands up. He's now out in the open, completely exposed. He closes his eyes tight, expecting the worst. They could gun him down right now. Drop him to the cold concrete, but they don't. Only sound is quiet. The only motion around him is the wind.

Detective Harris and Remo stare at one another. A chunk of open bridge separates them. A pack of armed friends stands ready behind each of them. Harris holds up his hand, letting his friends know to stand down. Remo does the same.

"Fuck that shit," Three Bills says. "Who the fuck made you Chief Dickhead?"

Lester puts him in a headlock and takes his gun away. He nods to Remo, letting him know that all's well.

Harris passes by a burning car as he walks toward the center of the bridge. Remo does the same. Remo takes in a deep breath, trying hard to find some sense of calm in all this madness. He's walking toward a cop who hates him and whom he hates equally. This cop has tried everything over the years to destroy Remo, and Remo has beaten Harris in court time and time again. Usually in a humiliating fashion.

The two get closer and closer. Seconds from meeting together alone, one-on-one, in the middle of the open space on the war-torn bridge. Cars burn around them. Shells and tire marks pepper the concrete floor of the bridge. Remo lets his thoughts bounce around the idea of bashing this asshole's head into the concrete and letting the two sides go into all-out battle mode. Let the guns decide the winner.

Remo reaches Harris.

They stand about a foot away from one another.

Eyes locked.

A lot of history here. None of it good.

Neither says a word for what seems like hours.

"Well?" Harris says.

"That's all you've got, Harris?" Remo raises his eyebrows. "You fucking kidding me?"

"What should I say?"

"I'm not sure, but I need a little more than *well*."

"How the hell did you get into this shitshow?"

"Well, Detective Harris, one might say it's because you sold my pale ass to CIA man Cormack."

Harris looks down at his feet, kicking at a spent shell casing.

"This. All this shit," Remo says. "It's the domino effect of you handing me off to that motherfucker."

"It happens."

"You're such a fucking stupid prick. How did you even find me at that airport?"

"Cormack had me put your name and face out with every officer in the state of New York. Every man and woman around. Every set of eyeballs. Every security camera. Everyone was supposed to be aware if you stepped one toe back into the state of New York. His words."

Remo rolls his eyes. He can't believe this shit. Cormack is killing him from the grave.

"You and your buddies got all the way into the city before I knew about it," Harris says. "Then I had someone tail you to that Jersey titty joint. I could tell something was up."

"Unbelievable."

"Look. Things got a little fucked up. Slightly out of control. I'll admit that."

"Ya think?"

"Cormack has me. Deep. I'm so boxed in with that guy I can't even tell you. What was I supposed to do? He's going to bury me under the prison."

It hits Remo. Harris has no idea that Cormack is dead. He doesn't know that Cormack is missing half his head, laid out in a garage at some not-so-safe house in the middle of nowhere

New Mexico. It's as if Remo's head actually makes a *ding* sound.

"What if I can work something out with Cormack?" Remo asks.

"What do you mean?"

"I mean I've got something. A lot of shit's happened since you saw me last."

"Apparently."

"I can control Cormack. I can call the dog off. I can get you well again."

"How?"

"Never mind how. I can guarantee you will never see or hear from Cormack again, but only if you help me out of this little pickle I'm in."

Harris looks around at the pack of killers behind Remo, and then back to his people, who are standing behind him, waiting for his orders. Remo can tell his mind is ripping at a hundred miles a second. Harris has no reason to trust Remo, but the very idea that Remo could help him is enough for Harris's desperate mind to consider the possibly. Lost souls are an easy sell, and Remo knows it. He pushes the pedal down on the conversation.

"I'll be honest, Harris. I have no idea what Cormack has on you, and I don't care. I need to get off this damn bridge." Remo resets, rubs his tongue over his teeth, then starts up again. "I need to get off this damn thing with a couple of people I've got over there. They're nothing to you. You can have the other three. You'll want the other three. They've got some pretty large ties. Could be a very good day for you. Get out from under Cormack and take down a big-ass bust."

Remo can tell he's got hooks deep into Harris. Harris has no real play here other than to work with Remo. He is completely fucked and they both know it. What does he have to lose?

"What do you want to do?" Harris asks.

"What do you mean?"

"About this. This situation."

"Oh." Remo thinks. He hadn't gotten that far. Squeezes his eyes tight, then says, "I can get Hollis, Lester and the other guy on board, but the other three might give me some static."

"We've got maybe a minute, two tops, before the entire world comes crashing down on us," Harris says. "This bridge looks more like Fallujah than New York state."

"If I can get the other three unarmed, down on the ground and hand them to you, can you guarantee me safe passage back to the city?"

"What?"

"I'll gift wrap you two goons who work for the Turkov brothers and some fat bastard who no doubt has ties to some large, big-ass criminal masterminds."

"Why, because he came in on a plane?"

Remo pauses. "Yes."

"And you want a ride to the city in exchange?"

"I want a car and for your trigger-happy assholes not to shoot me, Hollis, Lester or my other guy."

Now Harris stops to think. He turns back to the line of gun-wielding cops and vest boys behind him, then glances to Remo's side. Remo can see it in his eyes. He knows a cop's eyes better than anyone. It's as if Remo was reading a stop sign. Whatever is about to come out of Harris's mouth is a lie.

"Okay," Harris says. "You give me them with no blood loss and I'll get you into the city."

Remo's heart drops. He knows he's screwed in every direction, but at least he's got one side of this equation to stop shooting. Harris will at least not come charging in with guns blazing.

Maybe.

"But," Harris says, "you've got two minutes before I'm going have to take this bridge. I can't have this turn into a *Dog Day Afternoon* type deal all over the Internet. You got it?"

Remo's got it. He's got one hundred and twenty seconds before Harris comes charging in with guns blazing.

Remo nods.

Harris nods.

They both turn back to their sides.

CHAPTER SEVENTEEN

Remo settles in behind the Camry with Lester, Hollis and his other bloodthirsty traveling companions.

His brain passed fried hours ago, headed toward full-on meltdown, and left Remo with a quivering mass of jelly between his ears. He looks to his watch. Seconds are ticking fast. There's none to waste.

"Well?" Three Bills asks with a bit of a tone.

Lester and Hollis look Remo over. They know something is up here, but not sure what. With Remo, anything is possible.

Oleg and Poe grunt, their eyes dancing between the other side of the bridge and Remo. Remo sucks in a deep breath, letting it creep out slowly. Remo has to let Hollis and Lester know what's up, but at the same time he needs to maintain full control of the Oleg, Poe and Three Bills situation. There's no time for a private conversation. No sidebar.

Remo closes his eyes, shutting them tight as he can.

"You gonna fucking speak?" Three Bills pushes.

The seconds tick.

"What's with this guy?"

Tick.

Lester puts a calming hand on Remo's shoulder.

Remo remembers his conversation with Hollis and Lester and something he learned from that chat.

Tick.

Bullshitting the people close to you is not always a great idea. Sometimes, if not always, the truth is the clearest, simplest path to getting what you want. Certainly the easiest thing to remember.

Tick.

Remo's eyes flip open. He readies his Glock, gives a quick side-eye to Hollis and Lester. So slight the other three don't even notice.

"We're going to take you down, hand you over to the other side without an ounce of shit from any of you."

Lester lands a fist to Poe's jaw then lunges for his throat knocking him back.

Hollis slams the butt of his AR into Oleg's nose. In a single motion, he rips Oleg's gun out from his hand, letting it skid down the bridge, then pins him to the side of the Camry by jamming his rifle sideways under his chin. Oleg's veins bulge out from under the rifle.

Remo jams his Glock between Three Bills's teeth, slipping the AR from his fumbling sausage fingers. Turning his head to Hollis and Lester, Remo finally feels some sense of control.

Tick.

"We also need to jump off the bridge and then steal a car," Remo says. "Like in less than thirty seconds."

Hollis and Lester both shrug. This sort of thing happens.

They quickly use the zip ties they had from the airport job to secure Oleg and Poe. Remo pulls a pair of zip ties from his pocket so he can do the same with Three Bills. The fat man calls Remo a cocksucker about fifteen times. It was hard to make out through the gun barrel in his mouth, but Remo was able to translate after a while. Remo allows himself to breathe easier. That went a helluva lot smoother than he thought.

Three Bills pulls back hard and Remo's gun slips out from his lips. He tries his best to slap the gun away from Remo. The gun goes off. Three Bills's head pops like a melon dropped from a ten-story building. What's left of him slumps, then falls off to the side. His thick neck pulses crimson, spraying out on the bridge like a deranged sprinkler. Remo's eyes bulge wide like plates.

Tick.

"Remo?" Harris says through the bullhorn across the bridge.

"We're cool," Remo yells back, standing up waving his arms as if landing a plane. "Nothing to worry about over here."

Harris scrunches his nose. "Clock's still running."

Remo gives two big thumbs-up then slumps back down behind the Camry.

"Don't we need that guy?" Hollis says.

"Hope not," Lester says, with eyes on Three Bills.

"No shit," Remo says.

"No." Hollis grabs Remo by the ears, turning his head behind them. "That guy."

J. Slim has escaped out from the back of the Yukon.

Tick.

CHAPTER EIGHTEEN

"Shit," Remo yelps.

J. Slim stumble-runs, heading toward the 18-wheeler behind them. His legs are obviously not responding well after being knocked out and stuffed into the back of an SUV. Remo springs up to his feet, hauling ass toward J. Slim.

"Remo?" Harris calls out through the bullhorn.

Tick.

"Remo, goddammit!"

Remo ignores Harris's calls as his feet leave the bridge, lunging, landing NFL-style onto J. Slim's back. Piggyback-style, Remo twirls with arms wrapped around J. Slim's back, holding on for dear life. He's planted his face perfectly between the shoulder blades, like he was a human dart thrown by God. J. Slim twists then turns then spins around and round, eventually landing them both in a heap of flesh and bone onto the bridge's hard concrete floor.

J. Slim wiggles free, landing an elbow strike to Remo's face.

Remo's head jolts, whipping back then forward like his neck was a spring, only to be met by another strike to the face.

Remo throws a blind punch, reaching nothing but empty air.

He swings another. Nothing.

The third punch lands, tagging J. Slim square in the eye. Remo seizes the flash of a moment by contorting himself around, managing to get J. Slim in a headlock of sorts. It's not textbook, but it's working.

J. Slim stands, his strong legs lifting them both up with Remo still on his back, hanging on like a baby chimp. Slamming his back into the 18-wheeler, J. Slim is doing his damnedest to knock himself free from Remo's death grip. He slams again, again and again. Remo feels his back crack. The air leaving his lungs as his ribs crunch. Still he manages to hold on. But he knows it won't last. Through the haze of his failing fuzzy vision Remo can see what's unfolded up ahead near the Camry.

Poe is working hard to wrestle a gun away from Hollis, and Oleg has just kicked Lester in the skull, sending him falling backward. Oleg scramble-crawls toward an AR as fast as he can with his hands still zip tied.

Tick.

Another slam to Remo's back.

"Remo! We gotta wrap this up," Harris says through the bullhorn, pointing to the sky. "Hear that?"

Slam.

In the distance Remo can hear the helicopters. They're coming.

In this split second, Remo knows that Harris will never let this turn into a full-blown standoff video vomited all over social media for the masses to consume. He can't. It's going to be hard enough to explain why he was at the airport in the first place, let alone involved in this shit. It's going to be a massive challenge for Harris to talk his way around the eyewitnesses, but he can manage the message if he's smart. But if people—people meaning officials, FBI and the like—start digging too deep into this, it will all fall apart, and any value Harris would get for bagging Poe and Oleg will disappear fast. He doesn't even know that Three Bills is useless, on account of being deader than Dillinger.

"Shit," Remo says, defeated as hell.

Slam.

"Wait," Remo screams into J. Slim's ear. "Look. You see that shit?"

J. Slim stops. Up ahead he can see a line of cops and vest boys moving toward them. Guns raised and moving slowly but steadily toward them. They are using cars as cover, with the black sedans creeping ahead of them.

Hollis reaches Poe and punches the piss out of him. Poe has gotten hold of a gun, however.

Lester is now bashing Oleg's skull into the bridge. That won't last long.

J. Slim moves away from the 18-wheeler. As he does, he spins around, letting Remo flail while still holding on to his back. Behind them is another line of cops moving toward them from the other side.

J. Slim's face goes slack, resigning himself to the hopelessness of the situation he's woken up in. "Thoughts?" J. Slim asks, tilting his head back to Remo as he hangs there.

"I do." Remo resets. He knows he's got nothing, but he's got to keep working this thing as if he's got some cards left to play. "I know that cop, the one with the bullhorn. We can still be okay, but you have to tell me where that asshole has my ex and my son."

"Fuck you." J. Slim cracks a chuckle. "You really think I'm an idiot, don't you?"

"Fine. Take your chances. How do you think that cop over there knows my name? You think *Remo* was a lucky-ass guess?"

J. Slim's head is spinning and Remo can see it.

The lines of cops and vest boys are closing in from each side. Poe can now see them, and he raises his gun toward the cops. Bad idea. They carve him up with a stream of lead. Pops of gunfire rip him apart, starting at the head and moving down, leaving a meaty, bloody mess on the bridge.

Hollis spins away back behind the Camry for relative safety. He grabs Lester by the arm, dragging him away from what's left of Oleg. Remo locks eyes with Hollis and Lester.

Nothing said. Nothing to say.

Remo hopes silent mental communication is a thing.

"Gotta talk now or this goes horribly wrong for you, and I won't be able to help you," Remo says into J. Slim's ear. "What do you have to lose? This is just bad on top of bad." Remo slips from J. Slim's back, standing in front of him. Makes sure to hold eye contact. He doesn't have much time. There's a hint of fear in J. Slim's eyes. A crack in his armor. Remo presses on. "Anna and Sean have nothing to do with this. I'm the asshole. Me, only me, not them. Ray isn't going to gain anything by killing them." Remo waves his arms. "Look around. What the fuck am I going to do? How am I a threat anymore?"

J. Slim scans the bridge. They are completely boxed in. Nowhere to go, with an army of guns waiting to storm in. J. Slim begins to shake. This is the first time Remo has ever seen this man even vaguely concerned, let alone afraid.

J. Slim looks to Remo.

To the cops.

Back to Remo.

"You better not fuck me over," he says as he pulls a card from his back pocket. With a shaky hand, he hands it to Remo.

Remo snatches it and checks the back. There's an NYC address. He knows the neighborhood. It could easily match what Remo last saw on the iPad before it went black. He coughs, almost choking as he scans the address. He can't believe it worked. There's still a chance. He smiles huge.

"Thank you," Remo says, then nods to Hollis and Lester. "Now," Remo says to Hollis, then turns to J. Slim. "Go fuck yourself."

"What?" J. Slim stammers.

Hollis moves up quickly, jamming a Glock to the side of J. Slim's head. He pulls the trigger. Hollis and Remo both feel a sense of something undefined wash over them as J. Slim's brains blow out and his body slumps. Before his body even reaches the pavement, Remo, Lester and Hollis run hard toward the side of bridge.

"Remo!" Harris screams out.

The three remaining members of Mayhem Inc. jump off the bridge.

HOPE

Part III

CHAPTER NINETEEN

When you hit the water from that height, shit happens.

Remo read once if you jump from the Golden Gate Bridge you'll more than likely die from blunt-force trauma. Death isn't a slam dunk, but if he remembers correctly something like ninety plus percent of people die. Now, he doesn't have the specs, but he's fairly certain this bridge is not an exact match to the fall from the Golden Gate, but this is the kind of shit that floats through your head as you're floating through the air after having just jumped from a bridge.

He's pretty sure his ribs will break, but he's also pretty sure they are already broken. He's also positive an organ or two will come unhooked or relocated inside of him, but there's not a whole hell of a lot he can do at the moment.

That ship has sailed, as they say.

In that moment before he hits the water, he remembers a little something from his childhood. He remembers breaking into a rich kids' country club and taking turns with his drunk, dumbass friends jumping off the ten-meter platform. It was the highest thing he'd ever seen. None of boys were expert divers, but one had done that jump before and did have a tip for Remo as the terrified teen stood at the end of the platform looking down at the cold water below.

"Jump and keep your damn body straight," he told Remo with beer-soaked breath, "with your shit pointed at the water at all times."

"My shit?" Remo asked, with his voice shaking.

"Your toes, boy, keep your damn toes pointed at the water. And when you hit the water, stretch your legs and arms out and arch your back."

Then that wise, learned asshole pushed Remo off the platform.

Remo hits the water hard with toes straight as can be. He knows it's so damn cold, but his body hasn't caught on yet. He managed to get his legs stretched and arms somewhat out, but definitely got his back arched. With no idea how far down he's sunk, he starts to feel the momentum of the fall slowing. He levels his body and swims with all he has toward what he's sure is land.

Reaching the surface, he lets his head come up just enough to grab some air and not give too much of a visual. As his ears get above water he can hear the sounds from the bridge. A quick blip of sirens and helicopters behind him. He goes back down and thrusts his arms forward, then back. While he was up he did steal a quick glimpse of land up ahead. At least he got pointed in the right direction.

Remo has no idea where Lester and Hollis are at the moment. He hopes they are right alongside him. He knows this is nothing to Hollis. The man has trained for every possible shitty situation there is, and jumping from a bridge is like playing jump rope to him. No need to rely on a buried teenage memory for survival, like Remo. He's more concerned that Lester even knows how to swim. No military in his background that Remo can remember. A pure badass on dry land, but in the water Remo doesn't know. He hopes for the best.

Now he feels it.

Oh yeah, it's really fucking cold.

Remo lands on the shore. He spits out what feels like gallon after gallon of dank river water. His lungs burn. His eyes at first provide him nothing but a view of a blurry world, but then his vision starts to work again.

Turning back, he takes a look at the bridge. From here it looks even worse than before. From this vantage point he can see the traffic is backed up on each side. Looks like it stretches for miles. Smoke twists upward, dissipating as it ascends up into the sky. He can hear the scream of squad cars cutting through the gridlock as they work to get closer and closer to the post-warzone bridge. Multiple helicopters are now hovering above and circling the bridge. A quick count gives him a tally of five crowding the blue sky. Three look to be media related, the others cops and feds. He can barely make out the cops and vest boys who are scurrying all over the bridge, looking much like upright ants racing around their hill that's been attacked. An image of Harris discovering that his prize criminal busts are dead on the bridge and that Remo, Hollis and Lester have slipped through his dirty fingers makes Remo smile.

He even giggles to himself a little. It's the small victories in life.

A thick hand grabs the back of Remo's Kevlar vest, pulling him all the way out of the water. It's Lester. They lie on the ground side by side. They both suck in huge gulps of air, trying to find some feeling of normal. Their eyes almost hang from their skulls. Remo is sure he is damaged in ways he can't even count, but, at the moment, he feels somewhat okay. Or at least what passes for okay these days. His mind slaps back on the here and now.

What's important. His eyes flare.

Got to get to Anna and Sean.

"We need a car. Now," Remo gets out between breaths. He looks around. "Where's Hollis?"

Lester shakes his head.

"What?" Remo asks. Fear spikes as he asks, "Is he dead?"

"No. Shit, no. He's cool. He took off."

Relief rockets through Remo. The idea that Hollis would die in all this would be too much. It's an idea Remo has had to wrestle with the last few days. The idea that a friend of his would be hurt, or worse, because of him is something Remo doesn't want to be a part of. After the relief subsides, Remo thinks. Then gets pissed off.

"What the hell do you mean, *he took off?*"

Lester's eyes slip over to the bridge. The sounds of the sirens are intensifying even from this distance. The choppers' whirling from above is getting louder and louder. They are starting to scan the water. Scanning for them. Lester gets Remo to his feet and motions for him to stay low. He moves them both into the woods. Out of sight from the watchers from above.

"Won't be long before they do a full-on search for us," Lester explains as they work their way through the thick brush.

"Where the hell is Hollis?" Remo asks as a branch thwacks him hard in the face.

"He's a smart man. They will be looking for three of us. Three of us together will be easier to find. He's been talking about finding his family anyway, so he took a stack or two out of the bags during all the chaos and decided it was time to go."

"Fucker didn't even say goodbye."

"Didn't want to make it a thing."

"Make it a *thing?*"

"He's not the sort."

"Unbelievable."

"There's more, Remo." Lester stops, then shows Remo several stacks of cash. "I took a little myself."

Remo's eyes meet Lester's. Remo knows where this is going before the man says another word to him.

"You're a smart man too, aren't ya, Lester my boy?"

Lester nods, then hands Remo a stack. "Take this and go get your son. Get your family."

"My son, yes, but not really my family. Anna hates every molecule of me, but I get what you're trying to say."

Lester, with the warmest of eyes, holds Remo's face in his hands. Hands that have killed more people than he'd care to count. Hands that cut off Dutch Mashburn's head and carried it around New York. Hands that have saved Remo's sorry ass and that have performed many a selfless act. Lester holds Remo's eyes with his for what seems like forever. Then he simply asks, "Did I save you, asshole?"

A part of Remo melts.

His stomach balls up inside. A lump rises up into his throat.

Lester's mission of mercy: *Kill multiple motherfuckers. Save one asshole.* A mantra Lester has held onto from the moment he left prison until now. A perfect little philosophy that Lester has used to guide him through the last few days, and for which Remo cannot begin to thank him.

Lester has saved his life on more than one occasion. Remo would have been dead a long time ago if not for this man. Probably gunned down by the Mashburns in New York, and definitely shot to hell in the Hamptons if it weren't for Lester. Remo knows that isn't the kind of saving Lester is talking about.

It's never been made clear if Lester fully intended for Remo to become a Sunday regular, sit in the first pew type of churchgoer, or study up and slide into being a man of the cloth. Remo hopes Lester will settle for Remo being a moderately better human being. If even only slightly. He's been in self-preservation mode recently so it's tough to separate the good from the bad given all the killing and such, but Remo feels like he has indeed changed. Hard to quantify or give a solid example, but incrementally, yeah maybe, Remo has become a better person. Certainly he's come to value others. Some more than others. Some more than himself. Remo can't begin to thank Lester for all he's done for him.

So, yes, in a larger sense, Lester has saved the asshole they call Remo Cobb.

Remo cracks a tiny grin and simply nods at his friend's question, unable to come up with the proper words.

"Good," Lester says as he releases his hands from Remo's face. He takes the Glock from Remo's waistband, checks the clip, puts one in the chamber and hands it back to him. He points straight ahead, showing Remo a new path. "Head that way. You'll hit a road. Get a car. Use cash or the gun, whatever works for you." Lester turns and walks to the right, away from the direction he pointed out to Remo. "Go do what you have to do to get to your son. Maybe Anna will come around ... now that you're saved."

Remo's face drops. This doesn't process.

He can't believe Lester, of all people, is leaving him. They've only been reacquainted for a short amount of time, but Remo has grown attached to the man. His right hand. His silent, wise man. His protector.

"Where are you going?"

"Not sure."

Lester is almost out of sight, slowly being swallowed whole by the trees.

"You can't leave me."

"I can."

"I need your help, man."

"You don't, but your boy needs yours," Lester says as he slips away.

Remo's heart pounds out of his chest. He's been alone for major chunks of his life. For the longest time, he thought alone was what he needed to be. That's all changed. Changed rapidly and recently. He sure as shit hasn't been alone since all this violence and insanity started. Not since he began down that unpleasant road. Not since he decided to grow a conscience and take on the criminal underworld.

Now Remo is more than a little pissed that Hollis and Lester have left him. Those fuckers should have let him die in the beginning. It would have been better for everyone concerned. Remo knows that's bullshit, but it's not complete bullshit. He's not sure that he remembers all the levels or circles or whatever of grief, but he's sure he's ripping through them, and he wishes they would just hurry the fuck up.

Remo stands in the woods, all alone.

Fights to not feel abandoned by his friends. He knows they are right, but hates them for it. He's better, not perfect. Cut a guy some slack.

The sounds of the helicopters and sirens offer a muted soundtrack in the background. Remo knows he has to move if he's going to have a single chance in hell. Alone or with an army, he has to put one foot in front of the other and go undo what he's done. What he's done to Anna and Sean.

Anna will be angry, and rightfully so.

Sean will be afraid, and rightfully so.

Remo hopes like hell they will both, at least, learn to forgive him.

CHAPTER TWENTY

Remo pulls himself through the wilds of the New York State jungle.

Each step hurts like hell. Every breath is a labor of love.

Self-love. Self-preservation.

He's running—well, to be honest, he's trotting—at an elevated speed though the uneven brush and dirt. The pain is real. His teeth grind. Eyes water. The desire to get to Anna and Sean drags him, pushes and pulls him, toward a road that lies only a few feet ahead. Could be a small highway. Hard to tell. Remo simply does not care.

He needs to get a car. Has to get a car. Must get to the city now.

Every moment is important. Every second he's not there is a waste of time.

Remo rushes out from the trees as if being birthed from the woods. He storms through a ditch that takes one of his shoes with it. As if a stray dog had snapped it off his foot. Remo slogs his way to the edge of the road.

He waits. Staring at an empty road like a zombie. He slaps himself to stay in tune with the world that is quickly fading into the background. The pain, the lack of sleep, the emotional beating he's taken is seconds away from turning his lights out.

He slaps himself again.

He hears something. Something coming his way.

There's a single car driving toward him. Like an angel from heaven, an Audi is barreling his way. Not too far away, but far enough for Remo to get his head together and ready his Glock. Perfect, Remo thinks. He can get out there, scare the shit out of this clown, take the car and get gone without a whole scene getting started. He stands out in the middle of the road and raises his gun, leveling it on the Audi.

The brakes lock up. The Audi skids to a stop a few feet from Remo's quivering knees. Remo races over to the driver's side window rapping the barrel of the gun hard against the glass.

"Get the fuck out of the car," Remo screams. "I'm not going to hurt you, but I need this Audi. Like fucking now, bro."

The thirtysomething man has no idea what to do. Frozen by the sight of Remo, he grips the wheel at ten and two and can only stare up at the crazy, wet man with a gun. Remo gets frustrated. He has no time for this guy's bullshit fear. Yes, Remo was afraid of guns a few short days ago. Yes, outside of a courtroom Remo had never been near guns prior to a few days ago. But shit has changed, and Remo needs Audi Boy to get up and get the fuck out of that car. Remo tries to open the door.

It's locked.

"Open the damn door, man."

Audi Boy panics and slams down the gas. Tires rip, scream as the Audio pulls away. Remo, simply on instinct, fires a single shot. The bullet blasts out the rear tire, shredding it all to hell. The Audi slows, twists and turns, dropping off into the ditch.

"Shit," Remo mutters.

He runs over best he can with his gun pointed at the driver's door. The door flies open. The thirtysomething Audi Boy comes out with his hands up. Remo lowers his gun. The car is stuck. The rear bumper and tires are an inch or two off the ground. Not going anywhere.

"What the hell, man?" Remo yells. "All you had to do was get out of the damn car."

"I got scared," Audi Boy says.

"I wasn't going to do shit to you. Just wanted your ride." Remo turns, looking all around the road. "Now what? Huh?"

"Don't shoot me." Audi Boy pulls out his wallet. "I've got cash."

"Fuck your cash," Remo says, then stops turning around.

Another car is coming.

An orange car. A taxi.

Remo's eyes go wide as plates, then he snatches the wallet away from Audi Boy. He points his gun at Audi Boy, waving him back into his car that's jammed into the ditch.

"What? You're robbing me now?"

"I am," Remo says. "Get your dumbass back in that German sleigh ride."

Audi Boy slumps, then slides back into his car behind the wheel with hands still up. The cab is almost there. Remo taps his gun on the window, motioning for him to roll it down.

"Toss me that phone of yours," Remo says.

"Oh come on."

Remo plants the gun on his forehead. Audi Boy hands him the phone with great haste. Remo pulls his arm back and tosses the phone into the woods with all he has. It flips and wobbles, bouncing off a tree before skidding through the leaves, landing God knows where.

"You can get it when I'm gone." Remo puts the gun back into his waistband and covers it with his shirt. "Now, get your ass down."

Audi Boy obeys, scrunching down into his seat, out of sight. Remo moves back out into the road, waving the wallet.

The cab stops.

"Here." Remo jumps into the back of the cab then hands the driver the card J. Slim gave him. It's soaking wet and barely holding together, but readable. The condition of the card, along with water dripping from it, plus the overall near-death look that Remo is sporting, earns a concerned stare from the driver.

"Go." Remo flashes some cash. "Go real fucking fast."

CHAPTER TWENTY-ONE

The cab ride started out by staying within the confines of the law.

Remo threw a few fresh dollars at the driver.

There was slightly more speed added, but the gusto Remo wanted was lacking.

Then he threw in a lot of dollars.

The driver is now cutting and weaving through the city like a man on a mission. A man driving beyond logic and reason. A man ripping through the city like he had a gun to his head. Oddly enough he doesn't, but Remo did consider it. The driver jams the gas. Lock-stomps the brakes. Whips the wheel back and forth, slamming and tossing Remo around in every direction in the back of the cab. Remo's faceprint can be seen on the Plexiglas that separates the two of them. Remo counts at least four times he's nailed the damn thing.

Remo has faded in and out during the drive. Allowing his body to be thrown around without much of a struggle, while trying to conserve his strength. Strength he knows he'll need. He's about to face the toughest test of his life, and any and all available strength would be appreciated.

Everything he's been through up until now was to prepare

himself for this. Remo knows it. He's not a deeply religious person, nor is he really spiritual in any way shape or form, but he does, from time to time at least, think things do happen for a reason. All of the violence, stress, bodily harm, wanton destruction—all of it—has brought him to here, and he'll need all of that to get through whatever is in store for him. There is a bad, bad man with his ex-wife and son. He has to remove this man without an ounce of harm coming to Anna and Sean.

He has no idea how to do this.

Who would?

Remo knows who.

He gets pissed at Hollis again for abandoning him. A little pissed at Lester too, but at least he did a little tearful goodbye thing. It was nice. But that son of bitch Hollis just bolted without a damn word. What a fucker. Remo could really use a friend like Hollis right now. His experience. His advice. Hell, him. Remo swallows hard as his head races through all the possible *what ifs* of this situation.

What if there's more than one bad, bad man?

What if there is only one, and Remo can't beat him?

And, the worst *what if* of all, what if that bad, bad man has seen the news and has already killed them both and decided to split before the shit comes down on him?

This is the one that has Remo frozen.

His eyes are in a deep stare, looking into the void. To a place only he can see. He fingers his Glock. Works the dryness in his mouth with his even drier tongue. His hands are trembling uncontrollably. He squeezes his eyes tight as the images of the last few days whip and blur, tearing his mind's eye to shreds. A flip-book of blood and chaos. Bodies rising and falling. Guns blasting. Anger. Danger. Hearts pounding to the point of near failure. All the mental games won and lost. The unmistakable truth that all of it was because of Remo.

All because Remo made a decision after watching a grainy security video.

All because Remo has a son.

Remo clucks his tongue, letting all that sink in. Letting that truth bury itself, finding a home deep inside his broken brain.

Fuck it, Remo thinks. *It was worth it.*

All of it.

Well, all of it *will* be worth it if a few things happen. All of it will be worth it if, and it's a big damn *if,* if Remo can take down this bad, bad man and get Anna and Sean safe again.

Remo's fear is unbearable. The worst idea yet is that all of this could end up being for nothing. The very thought that those previously mentioned *what ifs* could come to be true would make all of this a waste. Void any good created. Not much more defeating than a human being risking it all for a complete waste of time.

No.

Wait, there is something far greater. The lost lives. The dead and the living. There's been a river of blood and a pile of broken lives that can be pointed to through all of this little adventure. That's an idea that doesn't sit well with Remo. Not by a damn sight.

The cab stops in front of a busted-up apartment building. Graffiti-covered. Dumped-over trash cans. Homeless laid out at the doorsteps. Windows covered with plywood.

"This is it, man," the driver says, scrunching his nose while double-checking the address on the card Remo gave him.

Remo's eyes open. He checks his gun. Hands the driver some cash.

"Yes. Yes, it is."

CHAPTER TWENTY-TWO

The building is the perfect place to house bad shit.

Remo's certain that more than a few people were killed, or at least maimed, here this morning alone. If Remo wanted to kidnap and hold some folks somewhere, this would be the place he'd choose, too. Nobody's going to ask questions here. Nobody is going to notice a scream in this neighborhood, or a gunshot or a stabbing. The cops sure as hell aren't coming into this building unless they absolutely have to.

Remo enters with great caution, stepping through a front door that's barely hanging on its hinges. There's a drunk beating his head against a wall in the lobby while arguing with someone who isn't there. A puddle of urine pooling around him. Down the hall are three teens who stop what they're doing long enough to take a good look at Remo. A good, hard look. Remo flashes his Glock, letting them get a good, hard look at that. They don't seem overly impressed, but decide it's not worth the effort to engage.

Remo takes to the stairs. The apartment number on the card J. Slim gave him reads three hundred and two. He takes a stab in the dark and decides the third floor is as good a starting place as any, but he takes each step as if he were navigating a minefield. As if death could pop up at any moment. His Glock is lowered by his side, but always at the ready. He's picked up some techniques by watching and listening to Hollis and Lester, but he's still far from Special Forces.

Reaching the third-floor landing, Remo can see a door marked by a three and a two, with an empty space between the numbers that looks like it held a zero at one time.

He takes in a deep breath.

Shakes his head hard side to side, trying to get his mind right. Once he feels like he's in a decent place, he releases the air from his lungs. His ribs ache off the simple act of breathing, but he doesn't give them much of a thought. Moving toward the door, quiet as a church mouse, he focuses on making as little movement as possible.

Nearing the door, he leans his back flat against a dirty wall directly to the right of the doorknob. He listens closely, hoping to get some kind of clue as to what's going on in there. He hears a TV. Children's show, best he can guess. There's high-pitched talking followed by rolling, exaggerated canned laughter. That's a good sign at least. Means there's a good chance there's a child in there, and that child is alive watching TV. Anything is possible, but Remo feels slightly better. He lets his fingers re-grip his Glock. He's been holding it so tightly that he lost feeling in parts of his hand.

He places his ear harder to the wall, trying to get a better listen inside. Muffled noises. A soup of sounds comprised of TV, air conditioning and pipes running. He does hear what could be footsteps, but still no voices speaking. His breathing quickens. Chest tightens. Time to do something.

He re-grips his Glock one last time.

Steps back. Remo has no great plan here. It's time to go in and he knows it. Time to take the last piece of advice Lester gave Remo.

Go do what you gotta do.

The *what ifs* are all done for now. Filed away.

Now it's all about the *what is,* and what is behind this damn door.

Remo raises his gun and kicks the door in with all he has.

The door explodes open, ripping apart the doorjamb and slamming the door back into the wall behind it. The knob punches a hole into the piece of shit wall. Remo charges inside hard with his Glock tracking the room. This is a level of focus he's never known before. Eyes scanning. Heart pounding. The place is small, but he doesn't see anyone in the area. He hears a TV playing in a bedroom to the side with the door closed. He can see light dancing under the door.

There's a flicker of something out the corner of his eye.

Remo whips himself around with his Glock leading the way.

The bad, bad, psycho man is facedown, motionless on the dirty carpet. At first glance, he seems to be resting peacefully, but there's something off about him. A major item of note. His head has been twisted around. Completely around. His chest is down on the floor with his mouth and bulging eyes wide open, staring blankly up at the ceiling.

Cloris sits at a card table in the corner of the room enjoying a sandwich.

She glances up at Remo, pauses, then gives him a casual, yet friendly wave.

CHAPTER TWENTY-THREE

"Where's Lester?" Cloris asks while choking down some ham.

Remo can't even begin to process what he's seeing in front of him. It shouldn't surprise him that Cloris was multiple steps ahead of him, but shock still rockets through every ounce of his being.

"Hello?" She waves again, annoyed by the lack of response she's receiving from Remo. She snaps her fingers. "Over here."

"He left." Remo finally gets some words out of his mouth. "We separated after the—after some things happened."

She shakes her head, taking another bite. "Well, shit." Cloris drops her sandwich, disgusted by what Remo just told her. She's clearly annoyed that she has wasted her time with all this here. She pushes herself away from the table with a hard shove. "Guess I'll go find his ass. Again."

She zips up a bag that's been sitting on the table. Remo caught a quick glance before she closed it up. It's stuffed with money and at least two guns. The bag she took off the Mashburn compound in New Mexico, no doubt. She moves toward the door, but not before thumping Remo in the balls.

Remo folds.

"Your ex and kid are fine. They're in the bedroom watching some dumb-as-shit TV program." She moves into the open doorway, but before she leaves: "You're welcome, fuckface."

Remo fights the flutter of nausea that Cloris's well-placed nut thump provided him. He sucks in a deep pull of air and stands up straight, then bends over again. He thinks of throwing up. Couldn't hurt at a time like this. Completely justified.

"Daddy?"

Remo spins around.

There he is. Remo can't believe it. His reason for all this is in the same room.

Remo can't fight it. The tears start slowly, then roll with reckless abandon. He shakes and falls to a knee, letting his gun fall to the floor. Sean runs to Remo, wrapping his arms tightly around his neck. Every inch of Remo screams in pain, but he doesn't care. He'll take that kind of hurt and more of the same to be right here, right now. This is the best moment of his life and Remo doesn't give a single damn about all the pain, mental and physical, he's endured to get here. He's getting a hug from his boy.

His first.

Ever.

Remo can't help it—the emotions roar out of him like a firehose. A surprising flood he didn't know existed inside of him, but he loves it. Letting go is freedom. He's a sobbing mess and he won't apologize to anyone for it. Sean still holds onto his dad's neck as he pulls back, getting a good look at the old man.

"You okay?" Sean asks, trying not to hurt his feelings, though Remo is clearly a disaster.

"No, but I'm getting better."

"Good." Sean smiles, then looks behind Remo at the twisted remains of the bad, bad man. "Aunt Cloris said he fell down."

The words *Aunt Cloris* have a nails-on-a-chalkboard kind of feel to them as they hit Remo's ears. He smiles, plays it off, tries to let go of the *Aunt Cloris* bit, then simply nods to his son's shining face. Remo has not a single clue how to address that or any of the shit Sean's seen or heard in the last few days. Can't even begin to explain what Remo's been through either. He knows one day he'll have to try, but for now? Remo only wants to soak up this moment as much as he can.

"Sean," Anna says from the doorway. Her face has escalated to a shade of Corvette red. She can barely contain the rage that is bubbling up within her body and soul. Remo freezes, as does Sean.

"Honey," she says to Sean through grinding teeth. "Honey, your father and I need to talk."

Sean looks to Remo.

Remo shakes his head *no,* hoping Sean will bail him out. Sean giggles.

No. No. No, Remo thinks. He'd rather fight all the Mashburns, Mr. Crow, Cormack, J. Slim, Godzilla and King Kong than have a *talk* with Anna right now.

CHAPTER TWENTY-FOUR

To suggest the police, FBI and CIA were sympathetic to Remo's situation would be a gross exaggeration.

They listened to what Remo had to say.

They were helpful, to a certain extent.

They offered a solution.

Against his better judgement, Remo told them the truth. All of it. He told them about the Mashburns, Crow, Cormack, J. Slim, the Turkovs and all the finer points of disaster in between. The Cormack conversation was the one that captured their attention the most, just as Remo thought it would.

Apparently there had been whispers around the agency for a while about Cormack and his operations. Standard office gossip. Watercooler talk and the like, just like any other large organization. Only with the CIA, these types of things carry a little more weight. Require a little more concern and care. Cormack was a fast riser and had a reputation for getting shit done, which meant his superiors didn't question much as long as Cormack kept making them look good. He did just that, until he came across a man named Remo Cobb.

Many people have gone down in that deep ocean.

Remo also discussed Detective Harris's involvement, but he didn't want to. The man did help him to a certain degree on the bridge, but Harris was in way too deep and had way too much baggage. Remo framed it all the best he could, but he held no illusions that life was going to be pleasant for Detective Harris.

It was a tense room. The room in which Remo spilled his guts and gave it all up to the powers that be. It was a massive relief to Remo to let it all out. To unload, to unpack the last few days. The last few years, really. They put him up at a swank hotel with armed guards on the floor. He'd never slept so good. He ordered room service, three carts' worth, and took a shower that lasted at least an hour and a half. This rest and recovery time allowed Remo to find the proper mindset to sit in a chair and give it all up for the cops and feds.

After three solid days of his tell-all session, Remo finally struck a deal.

A deal that he never thought he'd make in a million and five years.

The CIA told him that there are still dozens of criminal organizations that want Remo dead. Ray is still out in the wild, and has people on the street hunting for him night and day. The CIA can't get a completely accurate measure as to the real numbers of questionable people who are searching for Remo, but it's high to be sure.

As they spoke in that room, Remo could see his life and career pass before his eyes. It's cliché as hell, but it's true. His formative years in Cut N' Shoot Texas. His dick of an old man. Law school. Moving up at the firm and all the cases that he won, and the handful he lost. Most notably the one case he threw that started a chain reaction, that landed him in the interrogation hot seat.

The Mashburn case was the one that started a raging bonfire that continues to burn.

The deal Remo struck will protect him, or at least try to. In exchange for the information Remo has given and will continue to give, Remo will go into the program. His continuing information is more or less an evergreen fountain of details via an off-the-record hard drive Remo produced from his old firm. The *in case of emergency* hard drive he went through a lot of trouble to get before his original meeting with Cormack. Somehow the drive survived all the shit from the last couple of days, and Remo couldn't be more thankful. This treasure trove of information will help supply law enforcement for years to come. None of it admissible in a court of law, of course, but it's great stuff to build off of, and will not be spoken of again by Remo or anyone else.

Remo's only condition before being placed in the program?

He wanted to make sure Anna and Sean were also taken care of. If Ray and the other members of the criminal element wanted Remo dead, then it's not a stretch to think they would go after the two of them just like Ray and J. Slim did.

The solution is not picture perfect, but it works in a strange way.

Remo doesn't know the stats on the success of divorced couples in WITSEC, but he feels like it's what's best for them. Anna, Sean and Remo have been set up in the same town, but not living together. Remo lives a few blocks over from Anna and Sean. Remo wanted to make sure, wherever they ended up, that the school district was good, the weather was decent at least, and they were in a location that most criminals couldn't find if you spotted them the state and the first letter of the town.

They now have different names.

Hair colors have changed.

And they're alive and together. Somewhat.

Remo managed to find a bag or two of cash stashed at the house in New Mexico where he, Lester, Hollis and Cloris stayed the night of the chicken pepperoni incident. Remo conveniently left that house out of all the info he gave the feds. It was tricky, but he managed to stop by there before he went into protection.

That cash means that Remo can meet his healthy child support payment, and put Sean through college when the time comes.

Remo tends bar at a little beach place, and he loves it.

He sleeps with a gun under his pillow and an assault rifle in his closet. Anna and Sean's house is wired with more security equipment than Fort Knox.

Remo hopes Hollis found his family.

He hopes Lester finds whatever he's looking for.

He hopes Cloris never finds Lester.

He hopes Anna will forgive him and that Sean will adapt well to his new life.

For the first time in a long time, Remo has hope. Hope that the chaos is over. Hope for his family, as fragmented as it may be, and hope for the days to come.

Hope for better days, man.

That, folks, is all an asshole like Remo Cobb can want in this thing called life.

ALSO BY MIKE MCCRARY

Remo Cobb Series

Remo Went Rogue (Book 1)

Remo Went Down (Book 2)

Remo Went Wild (Book 3)

Steady Teddy Series

Steady Trouble (Book 1)

Steady Madness (Early 2018)

Stand Alone Books

Genuinely Dangerous

Getting Ugly

Mike McCrary's has been a screenwriter, a waiter, a securities trader, dishwasher, bartender, investment analyst and an unpaid Hollywood intern. He's quit corporate America, come back, been fired, been promoted, been fired again. Currently, he writes about questionable people who make questionable decisions.

Keep up with Mike at....

www.mikemccrary.com

mccrarynews@mikemccrary.com

5/22

Copyright © 2017 by Mike McCrary

Cover by JT Lindros

This is a work of fiction in which all names, characters, places and events are imaginary. Where names of actual celebrities, organizations and corporate entities are used, they're used for fictional purposes and don't constitute actual assertions of fact. No resemblance to anyone or anything real is intended, nor should it be inferred.

No part of this publication may be reproduced, stored in a retrieval system, or transmitted in any form by any means without the written consent of the publisher, with the exception of brief excerpts for the purpose of review or promotion.

Made in the USA
Middletown, DE
24 March 2018